THE HIGH WALL

Basil Copper

CHIVERS
THORNDIKE

This Large Print book is published by BBC Audiobooks Ltd, Bath, England and by Thorndike Press®, Waterville, Maine, USA.

Published in 2006 in the U.K. by arrangement with the Author.

Published in 2006 in the U.S. by arrangement with Basil Copper.

U.K. Hardcover ISBN 1–4056–3532–0 (Chivers Large Print)
U.K. Softcover   ISBN 1–4056–3533–9 (Camden Large Print)
U.S. Softcover   ISBN 0–7862–8147–2 (British Favorites)

The text of this Large Print edition is unabridged.
Other aspects of the book may vary from the original edition.

Set in 16 pt. New Times Roman.

Printed in Great Britain on acid-free paper.

British Library Cataloguing in Publication Data available

Library of Congress Cataloging-in-Publication Data

Copper, Basil.
    The high wall / by Basil Copper.
      p.   cm.
    "Thorndike Press large print British favorites."—T.p. verso.
    ISBN 0–7862–8147–2 (lg. print : sc : alk. paper)
    1. Faraday, Mike (Fictitious character)—Fiction. 2. Private investigators—California—Los Angeles—Fiction. 3. Los Angeles (Calif.)—Fiction. 4. California—Fiction. 5. Large type books.
I. Title.
PR6053.O658H54 2005
823'.914—dc22   2005021962

THE HIGH WALL

For
Richard Davis
Friend and Fellow Writer

CHAPTER ONE

1

It was one of those hot, humid days in L.A. when the sun shimmers off the asphalt and all one's energy is used up in devising ways of keeping alive until the comparative cool of the evening. This afternoon was no exception. Like always the air-conditioning in our building wasn't working and it was either suffocate with the windows closed or choke in the smog with them open. I'd chosen the latter.

I was standing by the window, watching the stalled traffic on the boulevard, conscious of the big patch of perspiration on the back of my shirt and wishing I'd taken up some other occupation. I get moments like that about twice a week in my racket so I don't take them too seriously. Stella was out for the moment so I didn't even have any coffee to look forward to. I looked up at the cracks in the ceiling and sighed.

I got tired of the smog and the traffic in the end and went back to my old broadtop. I incinerated a cigarette, put the matchstalk in the earthenware tray on the desk and put my size nines up on the blotter. I folded my hands over my lap and gave myself up to the contemplation of my navel. That was likely to lead to acid-stomach so I didn't stay there too long. I put my feet down again and took off my tie. I felt as crumpled as I must have looked.

I went out into our microscopic wash-room and was running a luke-warm tap over my head for the second time that afternoon when the phone buzzed. I didn't exactly exert myself getting over there and it had buzzed a few times more by the time I made it back to the desk.

'Faraday Investigations,' I said.

'About time,' a rusty voice snorted in my ear. 'I thought you'd gone to sleep.'

'I can't afford a rupture this weather for the rates I charge,' I said. 'What's your problem?'

The voice snorted again.

'You were recommended to me,' it said. 'Now I'm not so sure.'

'Please yourself,' I said. 'I'm not exactly busting a gut while these conditions last.'

'You can say that again, young man,' the voice went on frostily. I could feel the cool air coming across the wire right from where my caller was sitting. It made a change from baking smog.

'You must have had some reason for phoning me.' I said. 'You haven't gotten to it yet.'

The voice at the end of the wire went up another octave. I grinned.

'My name's Adelbert Fogel.'

'Are you telling me or apologizing?' I said.

A sharp yell came from the mouthpiece.

'Your manners are just what I've been told to expect,' Fogel yapped.

'You've been talking to somebody who knows me well,' I said. 'Let's cut the vaudeville dialogue and get down to it. What can I do for you?'

Fogel was breathing so heavily now I thought he'd had an asthma attack.

'I'd like to consult you, Mr Faraday,' he said. 'I can't speak over the phone. Are you free this afternoon?'

'As air,' I said. 'You want me to come to you or will you come over here?'

'What's the difference?' Fogel said suspiciously.

'None at all,' I said. 'Except in cost. It will cost you more if I come to you.'

The voice yapped again like I'd drawn blood.

'I'll come to you, Mr Faraday. Half an hour?'

'All right, Mr Fogel,' I said. 'I'll be waiting.'

I put the phone back and my tie on again. I went around the office clearing up. By the time I'd shuffled a few pieces of paper and straightened up the blotter I was in a lather of sweat. I sat down. Fifteen people in L.A. had died of dehydration in the last fortnight. I didn't intend to be one of them. I was still wondering who Mr Fogel was when Stella

3

came in. She had on a white outfit with a mini-skirt that set off her honey-coloured legs to perfection. The blonde bell of her hair shimmered in the brilliant shafts of sunlight that stencilled the blind-slats on the floor of the office. She looked at me with very blue eyes. I couldn't see a bead of perspiration anywhere on her perfectly groomed face.

'It's a little humid today, Mike,' she said.

'I provide all the comedy around here,' I said.

She grinned and put down a wicker shopping basket on the corner of her desk.

'Would you like some coffee or is it too hot?'

'I'd rather stand up to my neck in a bowl of iced fruit-salad but I'll settle for the coffee,' I said. 'It must be good for the pores.'

Stella smiled again. She went over to the alcove and I heard the click as she switched on the electric percolator. She came back while the coffee was brewing and unwrapped a package from her basket. She put something down on top of the bookshelf midway between our two desks. She bent down and fiddled with the floor-level lighting plug. There was a whirring noise and a blast of cooling air. I looked at the large fan with the white plastic blades which was chopping up the exhausted air as it moved in an arc between my desk and Stella's.

'Now why didn't I think of that?' I said.

4

'That's what you pay me for,' Stella said.

I went closer to the fan and turned round slowly, getting the full benefit.

'Before you spill over with gratitude,' Stella said. 'I ought to remind you it's coming out of petty cash.'

'In that case it ought to be permanently fixed in my direction,' I said.

'Scrooge,' Stella said happily.

She went back to the alcove and her percolating. I went and sat on my desk and tested the strength of the wind-drift. I glanced at my watch. Fogel would be here in a quarter of an hour.

'We got a client,' I told Stella.

'Oh,' she said.

She came and stood by the partition, keeping one eye on the coffee and the other on me. 'Since when?'

'Since about ten minutes ago,' I said. 'Character called Adelbert Fogel.'

'It's too hot to make jokes,' Stella said.

'I'm serious,' I told her. 'The name could be phoney, though.'

'As long as his money isn't,' Stella said. 'It's been a rough quarter.'

I grinned. I slid off the desk and sniffed the aroma of percolating coffee appreciatively.

'He sounds pretty mean,' I said. 'When I told him it would cost him if I came on over he said he'd come to me.'

Stella frowned as she finished pouring the

steaming fluid into the cups.

'It figures,' she said. 'We always get that sort. You'd better make sure he gives us a deposit in advance.'

I sat down in my chair as Stella put my full cup on the blotter. The sun, reflected off the surface of the boiling coffee, made little dancing patterns on the ceiling.

'He says he's already heard about me,' I said.

Stella put her own cup down on her desk and swivelled her chair to face me. I reached over and pushed the sugar bowl toward her.

'Who hasn't?' Stella said darkly. 'L.A. is a small place so far as that's concerned.'

'We'll know soon enough,' I said.

2

In the event it was more than an hour before Fogel showed. I heard the bell buzz in the waiting room and Stella went rat-tatting out. She came back a few moments later. Her face was pink and she shot me a strange, warning look.

'Mr Fogel,' she said.

She stood aside and a thin, emaciated wreck of a man creaked down the room toward my desk. I saw now why Stella was looking pink. She'd been trying hard not to laugh.

'These sort of young girls wouldn't have

done in my day, Mr Faraday,' the old boy grated.

'They'd have done in any day, Mr Fogel,' I said gallantly. 'But I gather that isn't why you're here.'

Fogel glowered at me glumly. He stood in front of my desk like he'd soon collapse if they didn't get some pit-props under him. His eyes twinkled shrewdly.

'Would you mind standing up, Mr Faraday.'

I stood up and looked searchingly at him. Fogel gazed up at me for a long moment.

'You'll do,' he grunted. 'You may sit down now.'

'I'll do all right, Mr Fogel,' I said. 'The question is whether you will. And you can sit down.'

Fogel coughed suspiciously and lowered himself into his chair. He put his heavy walking stick of yellow carved wood against the edge of the desk and looked hesitantly from me to Stella and then back again.

'I'd prefer to see you alone,' he said.

'The young lady stays,' I said. 'I have no secrets from her. Besides, we may wish to take notes.'

Fogel cleared his throat noisily.

'As you wish, Mr Faraday,' he said. 'It is, after all, your office.'

'Just so long as you don't forget that we'll get along fine,' I said.

I sat back in my chair and studied Fogel

7

carefully. He was an amazing sight. Of average height, his face was so lean and narrow it looked like a caricature. Grey-complexioned, he looked like he'd been carved out of old gnarled wood. In fact his head would have fitted better on his walking stick. I'd seen more realistic things in some marionette shows.

He had grey eyes set close together and his cheeks were always in motion like an animal chewing grass. His lips were a dour gash in his face and square, yellow teeth showed as he opened them. Every now and again he would draw his lips in with a rather deadly sucking noise. He had long sideboards that were probably trendy round about 1880 and his thinning white hair looked like steel-wool on top of his skull.

A pair of gold pince-nez were clamped across his red, beaky nose. Despite the heat he wore a pair of tattered grey wool mittens, from which his long, white, claw-like fingers protruded. His fingernails were none too clean either. I should have said he was about seventy but despite his decrepit air he could be sprightly when he liked. I found that out later.

He had cuts round his chin that looked like he'd been used to shaving with a blunt razor. It was the truth. I found that out later too. His clothes were the most remarkable thing about him. I'd noticed that he was wearing odd socks when he came in. His shoes were battered and scuffed and when he crossed his legs later in

the interview I could see that the stitching on his right shoe had burst. The laces were just pieces of ordinary string, broken and knotted together to hold the shoes to his feet.

He wore a suit of rusty bottle green that was darned and stitched all over with threads of many different colours. His name should have been Joseph. A musty smell like cleaning fluid or mothballs came up from him every time he changed position. He wore a tattered grey wool waistcoat, a black string tie and an old-fashioned celluloid collar. His black and white striped shirt was minutely darned too. Despite all this his voice was cultured and I saw the glint of a gold watch-chain across the expanse of his waistcoat.

'What are your rates, Mr Faraday?' he said in his rusty-tin voice.

I told him. He started like he'd been stung.

'As much as that?' he said.

'Why not save up and come back?' I said.

Stella had a sudden coughing fit at her desk behind. Fogel distorted his face into what was evidently supposed to be a smile. He wasn't making a very good job of it.

'And what would the advance be, Mr Faraday?'

'I haven't said I'll act for you yet, Mr Fogel,' I said. 'But if I did, thirty dollars would cover it.'

Fogel's eyebrows shot up.

'Remarkable,' he said.

'I guess it is on the low side,' I said.

A faint flush showed on Fogel's sallow cheeks.

'I meant remarkably high, Mr Faraday,' he snapped. 'I shall expect first-class service.'

'You'll get it, Mr Fogel,' I said, resisting a temptation to throw out the old boy on his ear. 'Now what can we do to help you?'

Fogel held up a mittened hand.

'Patience, Mr Faraday, patience,' he said. 'I have a card here. And your secretary can give me a receipt in the meantime.'

He got out a morocco leather wallet from somewhere in his clothes with a quick, shuffling movement. The wallet was secured with an old elastic band. He put down the thirty bucks like it was all the treasures of Arabia. His eyes followed Stella as she checked the money and went back to her own desk to write the receipt. I studied the slip of battered pasteboard Fogel had shoved on to my blotter. Judging by the printing style these had been held over from the 1880s too. I blinked. So far from being a drop-out, Fogel was apparently the senior partner of a law firm. Fogel, Fogel, Fogel and Fogel.

'I'll bet they have a hard time deciding which is which,' I said.

Fogel pursed up his lips. 'Alas, Mr Faraday,' he said, 'all gone except myself and my son. Brothers and cousins. One of the best firms in the city.'

'Still, it avoids confusion,' I said.

Fogel adjusted his pince-nez and shot me a crafty look.

'You might like to retain us in your tax affairs?' he said hopefully. 'Fogel is noted for its expertise in such fields. We could perhaps offset the expense of our services against your fee.'

Stella suddenly paused in her scribbling and gave me a wide, bright smile over Fogel's shoulder. I had a job to keep a straight face.

'I don't earn enough from this to pay tax, Mr Fogel,' I said. 'It's a sort of hobby.'

Fogel gave me a crooked half-smile and laid one clawlike finger along his nose. He looked around the office.

'Come now, Mr Faraday,' he said. 'You seem to be doing all right to me.'

He paused as Stella came across with the receipt. He held it up to his eyes and studied it carefully. Then he put it slowly into his wallet. I expected to see moths fly out but nothing happened. He secured the wallet with the elastic band and put the whole thing back somewhere inside his rusty green jacket.

'We seem to be getting off the point,' I said. 'You had a problem, I believe?'

Fogel cleared his throat with a rasp.

'I was coming to that,' he said. 'I own a tract of land up in the hills outside the city. It's about a two-hour drive. I'd like you to look up there.'

'With what purpose?' I said.

Fogel looked carefully over his shoulder like he suspected Stella was eavesdropping on our conversation. He started to lower his voice. I interrupted him.

'The young lady is part of this set-up,' I said. 'How's she going to take notes if she can't hear properly?'

Fogel had an ugly flush on his cheeks. Before he could reply Stella solved the problem. She brought her chair over and put it alongside my desk, across from me and the old boy.

'Now Mr Fogel won't have to strain his lungs,' she said brightly.

Fogel's pince-nez caught the light as he turned toward me again.

'Now, if I can get on,' he said. 'You were saying, Mr Faraday?'

'I'd like to know why I'm going up to this property,' I said.

Fogel gave his square yellow teeth a brief airing.

'Certainly, Mr Faraday. I was just coming to that. It's a small estate I inherited in the twenties. It's called Place of Hawks.'

He gave Stella the complete address with instructions how to get there and waited while she jotted it down.

'Very picturesque,' I said.

Fogel nodded. 'I haven't used it for years,' he said. 'But it must be quite valuable by

today's standards.'

'I wonder you don't rent it out,' I said.

Fogel looked at me sharply. The cunning expression was back on his face.

'There is a problem, Mr Faraday,' he said. 'A relative has been using it up until two years ago, when she unfortunately died. There's quite a large lodge and a stream, together with an area of woodland.'

'And the problem?' I said.

'I can't get up there very often,' Fogel said. 'The price of gasoline, you know.'

'You have a caretaker?' I said.

Fogel shook his head. I didn't ask him why. I knew the answers by now.

'I keep it locked,' he said. 'I haven't been up for six months or more. There's something funny going on there.'

'Like what?' I said.

'That's for you to find out,' Fogel said shortly.

He had an expression on his face like he'd scored a point.

'There must be something,' I said.

'There's a near neighbour on the mountain opposite,' Fogel said. 'Colonel Proctor. He phoned me a couple of times. He said he saw lights in the Place of Hawks. And there have been visitors in cars several times. He says he saw the cars and their tracks.'

'You got any game worth shooting?' I said.

Fogel shook his head.

'Proctor gave the impression it wasn't so ordinary as that,' he said.

'Can he see the house from where he lives?' I said.

Fogel shook his head.

'There's a magnificent view from his place but the lodge is hidden by trees. But there's lights stretching up the approach road and he would be able to see the house lights above the trees.'

'Might have been a fire in the woods somewhere,' I said.

Fogel shook his head.

'Proctor's certain about it. He drove up one night and made sure the lights on the road were on. Then he phoned up just to make sure it wasn't me. The phone rang but no one replied.'

I sat back in my swivel-chair and looked at Stella.

'It might take some time,' I said. 'I could call up there three, four times without spotting anything.'

Fogel looked alarmed for a moment.

'You could call on Proctor,' he said. 'He'll put you in the picture. And if he spots anything else he could phone you direct in L.A.'

'That's a good idea, Mike,' Stella said.

Fogel moistened his lips with a bluish tongue, looked from Stella to me.

'How about it, Mr Faraday?' he said.

14

He got up and held out an emaciated claw. I stood up too.

'It sounds interesting, Mr Fogel,' I said. 'Only don't expect too much.'

Fogel gave a rusty chuckle. It seemed to set the windows rattling.

'I don't expect anything, Mr Faraday,' he said. 'I been around too long.'

We shook hands. It was like tangling with a museum exhibit.

'I'll look up there tomorrow,' I said.

CHAPTER TWO

1

Adelbert Fogel had been exaggerating a little. It took me almost four hours to get to The Place of Hawks. But then he hadn't allowed for the cross-town and the freeway traffic. Probably because he hadn't been up there since the early twenties. In a dog-cart to save money. I was grinning so much at the notion that I almost missed the junction at the old turnpike.

The joke lasted me until I got up into the foothills. I parked in a layby and ate the sandwich and flask lunch I'd brought with me. That was Stella's idea. She figured there wouldn't be any places on the way. She was

15

right at that. The only pull-in was too near L.A. and much too early for lunch. It was a fine view up here and I got out my old powder-blue Buick and sat down on a big rock at one end of the layby and watched the few cars snaking up the bends below while I had my picnic.

The road swooped round in a series of spectacular hairpins between great outcrops of limestone up ahead and finally disappeared below the trees. The deep blue of the high hills began about ten miles farther on but I wouldn't be going that way. From what I figured I only had about five or six miles to go and I had to turn off on to a dirt road at some point. I re-filled my plastic beaker from my coffee flask, put my back against the rock and let my legs dangle in space.

I'd broken out the Smith-Wesson from the small armoury in my bedroom over at the Park West house I rented, and its bulk in the nylon shoulder holster made a reassuring pressure against my chest muscles as I leaned forward and demolished the last of the sandwiches. I started in on the home-made cookies Stella had packed for me and enjoyed a cigarette while I kept my eye on the road.

There was a hawk rising about a mile farther off, soaring and diving, using the warm air-currents to give him lift as he spiralled effortlessly upwards on his great wings. I watched him for about a quarter of an hour,

the sun hot on my face and shoulders, a cool breeze blowing around the bluff on which I was sitting. Sometimes the hawk dropped almost below the hard blue tree-line and then he would hover motionless as though searching for something, before getting in another up-current and going up perhaps two or three thousand feet.

I could have watched him all day but presently he got tired and went away and left me to the faint ribbon of road with the crawling cars, the firm blue line of the mountains beyond and the lonely hills. I finished off my cigarette and watched the last of the smoke scattered by the rising breeze. There was the faint tinkle of water somewhere from far away. It sure was one hell of a day for attending to business.

I looked at my watch. It was almost two o'clock. I poured the last of the coffee and screwed up the flask. I gathered up the debris of my lunch and carried it back to the Buick and stashed it on the back seat. There were a few fruit trucks passing down below on the way in to L.A., otherwise fairly light traffic, mostly private automobiles. I started up the Buick and crunched my way over the dusty gravel and back on to the road.

I was watching for the intersection. I drove on for a mile or so at a leisurely pace, letting the other stuff pass me, without seeing the turn I wanted. Presently I came to a heavy

17

girder bridge spanning a river. The thin thread of a waterfall fell perhaps a hundred feet down a tangled cliff-face before churning up the surface of a broad green pool. It looked like something out of a travel poster and I saw the State Tourist Board or perhaps some similar body had constructed a tarmac pull-up for cars on a rocky shelf facing the waterfall. There were three or four automobiles in there now and a fat character in a white suit and panama hat taking camera shots with a telephoto lens almost as big as himself.

I found the turn I wanted another half mile beyond the waterfall and turned off, the Buick's springs protesting over the rough surface. I drove uphill through thick trees for another mile and then the land dropped away into a sort of open valley. There was a bluff to my right and a big stone house set in a landscaped garden with a drive winding up the face of the cliff. That would be Colonel Proctor's place. I couldn't see any other houses around here. According to what Fogel had said his lodge would be roughly opposite.

I saw the drive-gates then and turned the Buick into the entrance. There was a high wooden and wire-netting fence about eight feet high with a padlocked bar across it. The place looked unkempt, with rank undergrowth and a pot-holed drive stretching for a hundred yards until it turned and was lost among the trees. A white notice board with faded black

paint said: PRIVATE PROPERTY. I got out the car and took the bunch of keys Fogel had left with me and walked on over to the gateway.

2

Fogel had tagged and labelled the keys for me. I got out one for the main gate and tried it in the big zinc padlock that held the rusty chain round the gate. It turned noiselessly and the chain fell back from the gate uprights. I frowned. The sun was hot on my back as I bent to pick up the padlock. Someone had oiled it recently. I tried the key two or three times more. There wasn't any resistance of the tumblers.

I looked around, my shadow heavy on the ground at my feet. Nothing moved in all the wide expanse of hillside opposite. I pushed one section of the gate back. It moved without a sound on the big iron hinges. I bolted the gate back on to the wooden block at the side of the drive and went over to the hinges. They'd been oiled too. The metal was shiny and bare of rust. If Fogel had been telling me the truth his six-monthly visits would hardly keep the gates in this condition. And he didn't employ a handyman on his own account. This was interesting.

I put the other wing of the gate back and

19

drove the Buick in up the drive. It was a melancholy sort of place. The thick bushes on either side of the pot-holed driveway were overgrown and neglected and made a sort of green tunnel which turned the afternoon sun into twilight. The air was warm and moist in here, like it was a tropical jungle and the beat of the Buick's motor reverberated and echoed back through the open car window until it seemed like an intrusion in the silence.

Once something like a snake writhed into the undergrowth at the side of the drive and as I came round the second of a series of sharp bends a rabbit scuttled across in front of the Buick's snout. I spotted something then and idled the car to a halt. There was a patch of mud up ahead in a spot which the sun didn't penetrate. It was about four feet out from the edge of the drive.

There was a score mark in the edge of it which might or might not have been caused by the passage of a tyre. It was too blurred and stirred up to let me be certain; I felt sweat trickling down my shoulder-blades. I lit a cigarette and fumigated a group of flies which had started dancing round my head. I flicked the match into the bushes and heard something scuttering away. I could hear all sorts of furtive animal noises above the quiet idling of the motor.

I went back to the car and reached out the sketch-map of the estate Fogel had also left

me. The road looped about for a long while before it reached the lodge. I saw there was another entrance which started in somewhere behind the house and joined a secondary road some miles farther on. Fogel had been too modest about the bounds of the place. I wondered why he'd never tried to exploit it. The timber rights alone would be worth a lot. I decided I'd look down the back road when I left.

I got in the car and put the sketch-plan in my pocket. I sat on for a minute or two, enjoying my cigarette and listening to the faint animal noises from the thicket. Presently I got tired of the humidity and the feeling of enclosure. I put the car in gear and went on bumping down the road. I was still travelling uphill but the vegetation was thinning out now. Then, suddenly, the trees fell away and I was circling a rough meadow where rank grass waved in the slight breeze and every kind of weed was flowering.

I guessed this had once been lawns and the hunch was confirmed when I saw the silent stone face of a statue gazing at me from out the sea of grass. The drive made a big U and I killed the motor and stopped in front of the house. It was quite something. Fogel's sparse description hadn't prepared me for the reality. It was a vast place, built in the Gothic style, of natural stone blocks quarried hereabouts, cemented together like it was MGM's idea of

mediaeval Europe. There was a big flight of steps in front of the central section of the house, which had two wings arcing out from it in the shape of a shallow U.

The front door wouldn't have been out of place in Chartres Cathedral and there was stained glass over the semi-circular window atop of it. Weeds were growing in the porch and the windows were caked with dust. There was a lot of ivy growing over the walls and the smell of decay. The drive looped around the façade and I could see another group of buildings beyond which looked like a stable wing.

I crunched my way down the drive, the sun hot on my head and the Smith-Wesson making an insistent pressure against my shoulder muscles. The house sat and watched me. I could see my reflections passing across the windows. It seemed like I'd been the only person there since the days when W. R. Hearst and Marion Davies came to tea. I reached the stables and looked around. They had red-tiled roofs, heavily overgrown with moss and partly fallen in. I tried the heavy wooden doors from which the weather had long since eroded all the paint. They gave but were securely locked and bolted. I went all down the row trying the doom, and then crossed the big, weed-covered courtyard, and checked the doors on the other side.

They were all locked as well. I lit another

cigarette and stood in the middle of the yard listening. I didn't know for exactly what. I got the impression there was some sound at the edge of my consciousness trying to make itself heard. But all I got was the creaking of wind in the trees and the sharp, insistent cries of birds. I got out Fogel's sketch-plan again. It looked like a photostat taken from the deed to the property. Everything was detailed, right down to measurements and the positions of the drains.

I looked round the yard again. There was a rusty iron grating set in the middle, probably for a car-wash in the old days. I saw then the moss had been disturbed for a couple of yards just before the drain grating. I went back over the courtyard toward the driveway. Someone had driven in the yard quite recently. The marks in the moss had been caused when the driver applied his brakes. More and more interesting. I flipped my spent cigarette butt down the grating and went on around to the front of the house.

The grass on the lawn waved in the breeze, occasionally submerging the grave face of the statue, and then clearing it. It was a weird effect like the stone face was playing peekaboo. I wouldn't care to hang around here at night. My footsteps crunched in the gravel and an animal screamed somewhere in the vibrant heat of the afternoon. I was beginning to understand why Fogel had never lived here.

I wondered how his relative had stuck it. Perhaps she'd had a companion and servants during her time here.

I went over to the Buick and wound down the windows to let some of the heat out. I got out the bunch of keys again and went over toward the front door. The key for that was a big thing and I began to feel like the Chief Turnkey at Alcatraz. This lock was oiled too and the big oak door went smoothly back on its hinges. I walked into the dim, cool interior, closing the door behind me. I waited for my eyes to adjust themselves to the light.

It was a sort of amber twilight, the daylight filtered through the heavy stained glass. The vast hall had a marble floor of black and white squares and there were lots of dead flowers sitting in big stone jars set about the floor. Somehow I didn't like that. It made the place seem like a funeral parlour. I went over to the nearest vase and rocked it slightly with my fingertips. There was a stale, foetid smell coming up from it and I realized it still contained a residue of dank water and rotted vegetation. Fogel had told me where to find the electricity and I made my way over to a door set in the base of the oak staircase.

There was an enormous fuseboard screwed to the stone wall inside and I threw the main switch. I closed up the cupboard and went back to the doorway. I flipped on one of the ornamental brass switches set alongside the

24

lintel and light gleamed in the lustres of a big chandelier suspended from the carved wooden ceiling. It was really rather a magnificent-looking place with lavish use of natural stone, rosewood and mahogany. The high tide of pre-First World War California interior decorating.

I figured someone should photograph the place for one of the architectural magazines before it was torn down. Or blew down. But as I continued my tour I realised there wasn't much chance of that. The Lodge was built to last. That was a misnomer too. There were four or five enormous reception rooms on the ground floor, two with huge fireplaces of natural stone. One room was a library with panelled walls but all the books had long been removed. There were some oil paintings discoloured with mildew and damp but which looked as though they might be valuable.

Most of the existing furniture was covered with dust sheets and a number of the carpets had been left half-rolled, like the occupants had been frightened by something and left in a hurry. The whole place was a puzzle. I couldn't imagine why an old skinflint like Fogel didn't realize his assets. The property must have been worth a fortune at one time and even now the buildings and fittings would have fetched a lot of money.

I left the ground floor and eased up the winding oak staircase. The treads were about three feet wide and the creaks it made would

have delighted Bela Lugosi. Up on the first floor it was even more fantastic. I could see up the stairwell and there were at least two more floors above this. And I hadn't ventured into the ground floor side wings yet. Fogel should have given me a guide as well as a ground plan while he was at it.

There was a faded gilt harpsichord at the head of the stairs and something like a panelled picture gallery that seemed about the length of three bowling alleys. The gallery was so wide you could have landed Concorde on it and still had room beyond the wing-tips. I tried a few of the bedrooms. Two even had four-posters. Probably reproductions but it was still impressive. There was a big question-mark here and I was nowhere near answering it.

I stood on the landing and watched dusty sunlight picking out the heavy embossed patterning on the ceiling paper of the stairwell. I was still standing there, thinking of nothing, when I heard a door slam somewhere on the ground floor.

CHAPTER THREE

1

A muscle fretted in my cheek. Normally, when I'm on a case I don't carry the Smith-Wesson.

Not unless there's a specific reason. I was glad I was carrying it today. Specially when I heard a door slam in a place like this. There wasn't a breath of wind outside. I looked at myself in a gilt oval mirror opposite. My smile looked a trifle crooked. Place of Hawks was living up to its decor.

'No ghosts need apply,' I said to myself, quoting Conan Doyle. I went down the stairs taking the treads two at a time. The front door was still closed. I worked my way through the main ground floor reception rooms without finding anything. Presently I pushed open a door I hadn't seen before. It led to the kitchen area. A tap dripped somewhere with a melancholy noise. It had all the ache of dead thoughts and dreams of all the people who'd ever lived in the place in it.

I went over to the shallow stone sink and tightened up the old brass tap. The dripping ceased. It was pretty dark in here so I put on the light. I had another surprise then. The room wasn't like the rest of the place. It had a clean, well-washed look about it. I saw then that there was a set of metal plates in the sink, like campers use. I went on over. There were scraps of half-eaten food on the plates.

I stood there, the sun from the dusty windows spilling across my face, and caught a faint whiff of something. It was unmistakable. Cooking smells two or three days old perhaps, but cooking smells just the same. I crossed to

the big, old-fashioned gas range. I tried the taps. Like I figured the gas was off at the main.

There was a row of brown-painted cupboards running the length of the kitchen on the side opposite the window. I opened the first one. That was full of nothing but air and cobwebs. I opened the bottom door underneath. A bundle of newspapers fell out into the room. I stooped to shove them back. My hand touched metal. I drew out a portable camping stove. There was a cylinder of butane gas in place underneath. There were three burners on the cooker. I replaced the stuff in the cupboard as I'd found it and stood up.

I opened up the next cupboard. There were two light aluminium fry-pans in there. They'd been washed and cleaned but the aroma still clung to them. Sausages and eggs I would have said. I tried the rest of the cupboards. Two were locked. In the third I found tinned food and stuff in plastic containers. There was enough in there to have kept the average person for months. I shut the doors again and stood frowning across at the sink.

It was then I heard what sounded like a faint footstep from far off in the house. Then a muffled noise like a door closing. I got out the kitchen and walked back through the house. All the rooms were empty and so far as I could see, all the half-open doors in the same position in which I'd left them. I got back in the hall and grimaced at the funereal flowers.

A shadow seemed to pass across the stained glass while I was standing there.

I opened the front door and got down the steps. There was nothing in the dazzling sunshine but the Buick standing baking on the drive and the waist-high grass stirring uneasily in the breeze beyond. I stood and smoked a cigarette to ease my jangled nerves. Then I went back in the hall and closed the door behind me.

'You're getting old, Faraday,' I said aloud. My voice had an unpleasant echo, that seemed to reverberate up and down the stairwell. I realized I'd made a mistake as soon as the words were out my mouth.

'It's the first sign of insanity,' I said. Aloud again. I grinned. At thirty-three you're beginning to crack, Faraday, I told myself. Not out loud this time. Whoever had used the kitchen, slammed the door and possibly passed across the front of the house was human, that was for sure. And that's what I'd come up here for. If someone was trespassing I had to find him. If I wanted to earn old Fogel's fee, that is. I stood listening for a whole five minutes but there wasn't another sound. I remembered the ground floor side wings then. I hadn't looked in either.

I padded across the hall and opened the first door. There was a solid stone wall of rendered blocks and the doorway had a Norman archway, with a big iron-bound door

set in it. The place seemed a lot older than the main house and I suddenly had the idea that the twenties part had been built on to match an ancient pile. Then I shrugged. This would have been all right in Europe but it wouldn't work up here. No one was building twelfth-century castles in the States. This would be Jazz-Age Gothic.

The key was in the door and I turned it. That moved smoothly in the lock as well. I opened up the door and found myself in a stone corridor. There were some woven tapestries on the wall here and as I walked down over the dusty stone flooring I could see there were a lot of marks in the dust. I bent down to examine them. It might have been mice. On the other hand it might not. In my experience mice don't wear rubber-soled shoes.

There were big dusty windows facing the concourse in front of the house so it wasn't too dark in here. There were doors set along the right-hand side of the corridor. I went down trying them. The first one I opened looked like some sort of store-room. There was a lot of lumber and junk hidden under canvas sheeting. The second looked like a harness room; there was tack hanging from pegs on the bare stone walls.

I tried the light switches in here but they were apparently on a different circuit and I couldn't get them to work. What light was

spilling in from the corridor gleamed on dusty brass ornaments and the collars of long-dead horses. I looked for the suits of armour but the prop-master had missed out on that one. The third door seemed more interesting. This room was rigged up like a gymnasium. There were white lines painted on the floor and equipment hanging from the ceiling.

There were two long windows punched in the opposite wall here and the light was much brighter. I walked on over into the centre of the floor, my footsteps echoing hollowly under the high arching. There was a long gallery with a wrought-iron staircase spiralling upward. The gallery ran round three sides of the room with the staircase snaking its way up the fourth wall.

I eased my way up the staircase, my progress rousing hollow metallic echoes from the iron rungs. I noted that the staircase was securely bolted into the solid stone wall with massive bolts. I'd seen too many films where spiral staircases gave way to miss that detail. The treads were solid enough. I got to the top at last and wandered a little way along the gallery.

The big windows went way up above the gallery level and I went over and peered through. I was directly over the stable area now, looking back into the courtyard where I'd been earlier. Nothing moved in the bright afternoon sun except the distant tops of trees

in the light breeze. I went back over to the balcony edge. This was made of heavy teak, smoothly shaped and oiled though long neglect had dried out the wood.

I wondered what occupant could have been so keen on physical culture that he'd installed all this; perhaps the building had been a school or some sort of military establishment at some period. I'd ask Fogel when I got back to the city. I was standing leaning on the balcony thinking of nothing in particular and looking down at the dusty patterning of the lines of the floor when I heard something that sounded like the distant jangling of a telephone.

I listened intently and then presently the sound was repeated. In all it rang about three times at short intervals. The noise died away. It might have been Fogel ringing up to see if I'd arrived. I frowned. Now I thought of it I sensed rather than remembered there had been a big old-fashioned stand instrument somewhere in the hall. But there was no point in busting a gut to rush back in there when the caller would probably have rung off long before.

Unless the call had been for the mysterious user of the kitchen? That was a point. I decided I'd wander back into the main house and see if anything was happening.

I was just about to turn away from the balcony when there came a sudden, insistent thumping noise. A shadow crawled across the

floor down below. The big, dark rubber ball bounced two or three times more and then came to a halt. A dry, rasping chuckle split the silence of the gymnasium.

2

The shadow crawled forward, joined up with some feet. A tall, solidly built man looked up at me mockingly.

'I hope I didn't startle you,' he said.

'Not at all,' I said. 'Glad of the company.'

I walked back along the balcony and got down the spiral staircase. The gymnasium echoed as the big man tramped down to meet me. I guessed the old place hadn't had so much company in years. Another dry chuckle sounded as I got on the ground floor. The big man gave me a hard, chunky fist to shake.

'I must apologize, sir,' he said. 'It was probably a silly trick but I wanted to see your reaction.'

'My nerves are pretty steady,' I said.

'So I see,' the big man said, looking at me shrewdly. 'Allow me to introduce myself. My name's Proctor. I'm Mr Fogel's neighbour up on the height there. He said someone would be up shortly to look around the property.'

'Mike Faraday,' I said. 'You're the Colonel Proctor Mr Fogel spoke about.'

Proctor gave me another long look.

'That's correct, Mr Faraday,' he said easily. 'Glad to know you, sir.'

Proctor was a big man; about six feet one or two, I should have said. I'm six feet three and he was a shade under my height. He was around fifty and had bushy, thick-rooted hair which was just beginning to be tinged with grey at the edges. His face was strong, with prominent cheek-bones. Though he was of heavy build his face was quite lean and narrowed at the chin, which had a deep cleft in it. He had strong white teeth and an old briar pipe protruded from them, sending up a thin wisp of fragrant smoke to the high ceiling of the gymnasium.

His face was red and raw, particularly about the cheek-bones, like he was out in the wind a great deal. Later I found he did a lot of sailing at week-ends. He had a thick black mustache and deep-carved lines at the corners of his mouth. His eyebrows were quite white, which gave his face a somewhat startling look and his eyes were a faded blue colour, like he was used to gazing at far horizons.

He wore a light-weight grey suit which had country connotations to my mind; the sleeves had much-worn leather edging at the cuffs and strong leather patches at the elbow. He had some fish-hooks stuck into the lapel of his jacket and a red silk handkerchief sprawled from the breast-pocket. His feet were encased in strong tan hunting boots and he wore pale

green socks over his trouser cuffs; one doesn't see that kind of rig-out in California very often and it made him look very English, like something out of an old hunting print.

His hands were very big and red and raw-looking and he carried a Tyrolean-style shooting hat in his right hand, which had a lot of feathers and fish-hooks and stuff in the band. Despite the heat he wore a pale yellow waistcoat and a red and green striped tie which looked like club or regimental colours. Yet he wasn't English; his accent had something of the South in it. He stood quite at ease, staring round the gymnasium as though we were both very much at home there.

'I saw your car drive up,' he said with another dry chuckle. 'And I took the liberty of coming on over. I saw you unlock the gate so I presumed you were from Mr Fogel.'

'You must have pretty good eyes,' I said.

Colonel Proctor slewed one brown boot on the wooden floor and stared sombrely at his toe-cap.

'I have a powerful telescope up there,' he said. 'It's one of my hobbies. Bird-watching and such-like.'

'It comes in handy too when Fogel has unexpected visitors,' I said.

The Colonel shot me a wry look from under his white eyebrows.

'Please don't think I'm a nosy character, Mr Faraday,' he said. 'But it's pretty lonely up

35

here. I live with my sister and we have just the housekeeper. So anything which might seem trivial to you—like a stranger driving up—is an event out here.'

'Sure,' I said. 'No offence taken. Was that you I heard earlier on?'

A strange expression passed across the Colonel's face.

'I don't quite understand, Mr Faraday.'

'I heard footsteps,' I said. 'And doors slamming.'

Proctor shook his head. There was a worried look in his eyes.

'I've only just arrived,' he said. 'I left my car in the drive and walked up. Is something wrong?'

'Nothing important,' I said. 'I could have been mistaken.'

The Colonel consulted a heavy gold wristlet watch.

'Can I offer you some refreshment?' he said. 'It's about the hour.'

I looked round the gymnasium.

'I'll finish up here later,' I told him.

I turned back to Proctor.

'That would be very acceptable,' I said.

CHAPTER FOUR

1

The Colonel waited while I locked the front door behind me. Then we walked back down the drive together.

'Have you known Mr Fogel long?' I said.

Proctor screwed up his white eyebrows.

'About ten years,' he said. 'I knew him in L.A. when I was in business there. When I wanted a quiet retreat he suggested this spot. In fact, he sold me the land on which my house is built.'

We were nearing the end of the series of bends in the drive and there was the glint of sun on blue metal through the trees.

'You certainly got a quiet spot,' I said.

We were round the bend now. Proctor climbed into the driving seat of the blue Rolls-Royce Silver Cloud coupé that seemed to fill all the driveway. I saw it was an English model, with right-hand drive. I got in the passenger seat while Proctor reversed gingerly back until he came to a place where the trees fell away, leaving him a space to turn around in.

The big car purred forward down the drive, the springing making light work of the bumps and pot-holes. I sat with the smell of expensive hide and tobacco smoke in my nostrils and

wondered when I'd be able to afford to trade in the Buick for a clapped-out Chevy. Proctor smiled thinly, his teeth clamped round the stem of his pipe.

'I see you don't impress easily, Mr Faraday,' he said.

'I impress all right,' I said. 'This is a lot of motor.'

'Don't get me wrong,' Proctor said. 'I'm not a rich man. I just love good automobiles. I got this one for next to nothing, traded in for bad debts on a company in L.A. which owed us money. I was lucky.'

'You certainly were,' I said.

Proctor grinned.

'My sister and I save up for weeks for a tankful of gas before we can afford to go anywhere,' he said.

I didn't answer that. It wasn't that I disbelieved him but the place on the top of the hill opposite didn't exactly strike me as the residence of a man who was short of change. Proctor eased the coupé across the road and into a lane almost facing the gates of Place of Hawks. We climbed swiftly round a series of S-bends in the private road cut into the cliff-face which led to his property.

The big stone house set in an acre or two of lawns sat shining serenely in the sun on top of the bluff. It wasn't on the same scale as Fogel's layout but then it didn't need to be. The Colonel tooled the coupé smoothly round the

38

last bend and crunched on to a gravelled concourse that lay below the terrace of the house proper. There was a garage block tunnelled into the hillside at the end. He pulled the Rolls up next to a white mini that baked in the sun in front of the house. Proctor got out the car with a wry smile.

'That thing belongs to my sister,' he said. 'We usually go everywhere in it.'

'A bit more practical,' I said.

'You should try it on long runs up in this country,' Proctor said. 'It's a young man's car. I prefer something a little more expansive at my age.'

He took a brown leather case off one of the back seats of the Rolls and led the way up a set of rough stone steps smothered with flowers and ivy. We got up on to the terrace where some wicker chairs and tables were set about.

The terrace, of pink and white stone blocks, was about forty yards long. It was divided from the house by another strip of grass. A big black telescope on a metal stand stood up at one end. It pointed down toward the gateway of Place of Hawks. There was a fine view up here and the secondary road looped away among the hills until it was lost in the dim blue of the mountains.

'Nice, isn't it?' said the Colonel, as though he could figure what I was thinking.

'Just great,' I said.

Proctor looked round, indicating the cane

chairs.

'If you'll excuse me a moment, Mr Faraday,' he said. 'I'll see what we can offer in the way of tea.'

'Don't put yourself out,' I said.

The Colonel smiled benevolently. He took his pipe out of his mouth and emitted a cloud of fragrant blue smoke.

'No trouble at all,' he said.

He went away across the lawn as I strolled down the terrace toward the telescope. I saw a woman waiting in front of the French windows up at the house. She kissed Proctor affectionately as he came up with her so I guessed she was the sister he'd spoken of. Or it might have been the housekeeper. It depended what sort of household it was. I grinned to myself. I looked back and saw that Proctor had disappeared. It was very peaceful up here; nothing but the shrilling of insects and the contented chirping of birds.

A big black and white cat was lying sunning himself on the tiles where the shadows of the nearest trees brushed the terrace. He looked at me with unblinking yellow eyes and extended a massive paw as I came up toward the telescope. I introduced myself and ran my hand along the side of his jaw. He stood that for about a minute or so and then indicated his boredom by slightly shifting his position.

I stood up and put the eyepiece of the telescope to my cheek. The instrument was a

heavy one and I found it had been locked in position. I had to readjust the focus to allow for my own eyesight. The area round the main gate of Place of Hawks sprang into sharp precision; there was a faint bluish halo round the images like there always is in first-class instruments. The telescope was so powerful that I could read every detail of the notice-board. I noticed something else too.

The name of the house was carved on a big oak shingle which was suspended from a post to one side of the gate. It was partly overgrown by foliage which was probably why I hadn't spotted it when I drove up. I looked at my watch. It was already turned four o'clock. I would have to leave at six if I wanted to get back to L.A. at a reasonable time.

I felt something brush against my legs. The cat was expressing his approval. A shadow fell across the tiling.

'You must have something special about you, Mr Faraday. Jake doesn't usually take to strangers.'

2

The woman who stood at the centre of the terrace was about forty-five; tall, elegant, with greying hair which had been fashionably tinted, she must have been a great beauty when she was young. She wasn't half bad now,

come to think of it. I took in the rest of her figure as she walked across over to me. She was carrying a heavy silver tray with legs like those things Eric Blore and Arthur Treacher used to carry in all those thirties movies.

She had good legs and a taut waist and she moved like she might have been a model. I guessed she kept herself in good trim. I could see the netting of a tennis court protruding from behind an angle of the house. My hostess smiled as she came closer, like she knew what I was thinking.

'It's kind of you to say so,' I said, answering her question. 'I've always liked cats.'

'They know it, of course,' the woman smiled. She had beautiful teeth that reminded me of Scandinavian women. She put down the tray on top of a wicker table and straightened up.

'I'm Helen,' she said. 'The Colonel's sister.'

I could see the Colonel now, stamping back out of the house like he was afraid to leave us alone too long.

'Glad to know you, Miss Proctor,' I said.

The tall woman smiled again.

'Mrs James,' she corrected me gently. 'We're divorced now, thank God.'

She wrinkled up her nose and bent over the silver tray again. 'It didn't take,' she went on. 'Life's a lot quieter and more worthwhile.'

She turned before I could reply and waited for the Colonel to come up.

'I see you two have introduced yourselves,' he said jovially. 'We don't stand on ceremony here.'

He frowned down at the tray.

'Even so, Helen, I think you might have let Caroline attend to that. She's younger and stronger than either of us.'

'Don't fuss, Henry,' the tall woman said. 'She's down in the kitchen garden picking fruit. I didn't want to drag her all the way up here.'

She turned back to me.

'I hope you'll meet Caroline before you go, Mr Faraday. She's a real treasure.'

The Colonel raised his eyebrows and shot an enigmatic look at me over his sister's shoulder.

'Let's all sit down,' he rumbled. 'No sense standing about in this heat.'

I dropped into one of the cane chairs while Proctor went to drag over a big blue sunshade in a plastic stand. He grunted with the exertion, adjusted its angle under his sister's direction. Mrs James fussed about with tongs and lemon and sugar.

'I wish you'd put that smelly pipe out, Henry,' she said fastidiously. 'It'll spoil Mr Faraday's tea.'

The Colonel gave me another curious glance.

'Sorry, old chap,' he said.

He took his pipe out of his mouth and put it

down on the terrace about three yards away. The smoke from its bowl went straight up in the still air. Proctor sank heavily into another chair opposite me. Mrs James was on my right now, pouring from a silver teapot.

'Hope you like the tea habit,' Proctor grunted. 'Can't do without it myself. Something I initiated at my business and I've stuck to it ever since.'

'Very pleasant,' I said. 'Especially in these surroundings.'

'I see you're a man who appreciates elegance in life,' the tall woman said, passing a steaming cup to her brother.

'When I can get it,' I said.

'Which reminds me,' Proctor said. 'I was surprised to hear that Fogel was taking this up officially.'

'I don't quite understand,' I said.

I took the china cup Mrs James handed to me and put it down next to my plate. She put two small sandwiches on the plate with a pair of silver tongs, together with a selection of savouries.

'It will save time,' she said with a thin smile.

'Your presence here, Mr Faraday,' Proctor said. 'I'm sure you won't mind me mentioning money but old Adelbert isn't exactly known for his outstanding generosity.'

He grinned suddenly and bit into one of his sister's small sandwiches with anticipation.

'You mean you're surprised he hired me,' I

said.

'Frankly, yes,' Proctor said.

'It does seem out of character now that you mention it,' I said. 'But perhaps he figured that if anyone was stealing from his property my fees would save him money in the long run.'

The brother and sister exchanged a wordless glance before Proctor went on.

'That could be the reason, Mr Faraday. Though when I reported to the old man I thought he might come up himself or perhaps engage a caretaker.'

'Just exactly what did you see, Colonel?' I said.

'There were two occasions,' Mrs James said gravely. She took my cup from me and re-filled it from the silver pot. I stretched out in my chair and looked down toward Place of Hawks trying to imagine what Proctor could have seen at night that would have prompted him to contact Fogel. Though he probably could have seen quite a lot with his telescope.

'I first drew it to Henry's attention,' Mrs James went on. 'I'd been sitting out here a month or so ago when a car drove up on the road and stopped. I could see the lights quite clearly. Then someone opened the gate and the car went up off the drive.'

'You couldn't see who it was?' I said.

The elegant woman shook her head.

'The telescope wasn't out here then,' she said. 'Henry normally keeps it in his study. But

I could see lights on at the house. They were on for about two hours. The car had gone again before Henry came home.'

'Interesting,' I said. 'Did you check the house?'

'Not immediately,' Mrs James said.

'I stopped next day when I drove by,' Proctor interrupted. 'The gate was closed and locked and there didn't seem to have been any tampering with the padlock. My first reaction was that Fogel or someone authorized by him had been checking on the place.'

I turned to look at Mrs James who was pouring tea for herself.

'What happened next?' I said.

'About a week later we were both here,' she said. 'Henry and I were eating on the terrace. That was when he got the telescope. Another car or the same one. And lights at the house again.'

'You didn't go down?' I said.

The Colonel shook his head.

'It didn't really seem our business,' he said. 'But I telephoned Fogel the next day. And he seemed quite concerned about it.'

'So you decided to keep your eyes peeled,' I said.

Proctor nodded.

'But of course, nothing happened after that. Leastways, nothing important. I kept watch from the terrace. Then one afternoon, about a week ago I was coming along when a car drove

out the entrance of Place of Hawks and went away pretty fast.'

'You couldn't see who was in it?' I said.

The Colonel shook his head.

'Too far away. And there was sun-shimmer on the windshield.'

'That was when Fogel decided to call me in,' I said.

'Henry rang him straight away,' Mrs James said. 'He felt he ought to get someone to look into it properly.'

She gave me a dazzling smile and started ladling cakes on to my plate. I settled down under the umbrella and stretched my legs and felt this was the sort of assignment that wasn't too hard to take.

'You've looked round Place of Hawks, Mr Faraday,' Mrs James said. 'What do you think of it?'

'Strange you should ask that, Mrs James,' I said. 'I've been wondering about the place ever since I arrived. How could a man like Fogel keep it empty like that? It's only deteriorating. It must be worth a fortune on the market.'

Colonel Proctor and his sister exchanged another enigmatic glance.

'We've thought about that too, Mr Faraday,' Proctor said. 'That'll be something for you to figure out if you're on the job long enough.'

'How did you get to know Fogel?' I said.

Proctor grunted.

'The old boy did some legal business for my

47

firm from time to time. He's a pretty good lawyer. When I retired we kept in touch.'

'I see,' I said.

I held up my cup and Mrs James took it for a second refill.

'What do you aim to do, Mr Faraday?' Proctor said. 'Have you come to any conclusions?'

'Too early,' I said. 'All I can do is poke around and hope something breaks. If the car turns up again I'd appreciate a call from you.'

I pushed one of my business cards across the wicker table to Proctor. He studied it for a long moment, screwing up his eyes.

'Will do, Mr Faraday,' he said.

'If you could get the car number with that thing,' I said, pointing to the telescope, 'it would be a great help. I could trace the owner.'

'Sure, Mr Faraday,' Proctor said. 'Anything we can do to help.'

There was a clatter up on the terrace behind us. Mrs James turned, a smile of pleasure on her face.

'Ah, here's Caroline,' she said. 'I'd like you to meet her.'

CHAPTER FIVE

The girl who came down the terrace toward us was really something. She was about twenty-six years old and she walked like a Greek goddess. She wore faded blue shorts and her long brown legs seemed to keep on going for ever. Her taut breasts strained forward against the thin tartan shirt, and a gold chain suspending some sort of medallion bounced lightly against her body as she walked. She had the sort of throat that looked as though it had been sculptured.

There was a deep cleavage revealed by the low buttoning of the shirt and her tan seemed to go all the way down. She was almost up to us now and I got to my feet. The Colonel and his sister remained seated. Now she was close I could see the girl had classic Scandinavian features. Her eyes were wide and cornflower blue; her brow was high and unwrinkled; her long brown hair, sleek and shining with health was tied in a pony-tail and flowed back down over her shoulders.

She had a retroussé nose, some of the longest natural eye-lashes I'd ever seen. Her lips were full and tempting and her smile as she came up to greet Mrs James felt like a 300 kilowatt lamp. I could have fallen in love with her on the spot. I was watching Proctor closely

and I read the expression in his eyes correctly. To my surprise the girl put her arms round Mrs James' shoulders and kissed her affectionately.

She gave me a wide smile. The gold bracelets round her wrists jangled as she came forward to shake me by the hand.

'This is Mr Faraday, Caroline,' Proctor said.

The girl dazzled me again.

'Pleased to know you, Mr Faraday.'

She sat down in a quick, supple movement next to Mrs James and put down a basket half-full of peaches on the terrace near her feet. I sat down too and looked across at Proctor.

'This is your housekeeper?' I said.

Mrs James smiled lazily and turned to the girl, passing her a cup of tea.

'This is the modern age, Mr Faraday,' Proctor said. 'Caroline is an au pair really. She's still perfecting her English. But she looks after us nicely.'

'Beautifully,' Mrs James said, using the tongs to fill a plate for the girl. I saw a secret glance pass between her and Caroline. Proctor intercepted it too. A dull flush came and went on his already fiery features.

'You are here for a visit, yes,' the girl said hesitantly, addressing me directly for the first time. Her eyes were so blue I had the impression I could look right through into her mind.

'Just for an hour or so,' I said.

The girl pouted.

'That's a pity,' she said, turning to look at Mrs James over her shoulder. 'It's so dull up here and new company is always welcome.'

For some reason that remark seemed to annoy Mrs James. I could see her elegant profile turn away brusquely. She rattled the teacups irritably as she gathered up the debris of the tea-table.

'You're late, Caroline,' she snapped. 'We expected you before now.'

The girl ignored the remark. She turned back to me, crossing one long brown leg over the other. She balanced her plate of cookies in her lap and munched with very white teeth. Her tongue looked as pink and inviting as a strawberry. I put down my cup on the table. I guessed the heat was getting to me. I was aware too of the deep cleavage between the girl's breasts. She seemed fully conscious of the effect she was causing and she shot a little smile across at Proctor. I guess there must have been a hint of malice in it I couldn't read, because he shifted uncomfortably.

'I guess I ought to be moving,' I said. 'It's a long drive back.'

'You're from L.A., Mr Faraday?' the girl said.

I nodded. Caroline turned the bright blue searchlights on me again.

'I'd like to visit there again, some time,' she said. 'I don't often get in. Perhaps you could

show me the sights.'

'Perhaps,' I said.

There was a definite atmosphere on the terrace now, that was strange and indefinable; there was a tension between the three people who lived in the house and somehow I guessed I was the cause of it. The girl was the centre, but without their knowledge I couldn't read the signs. If it didn't sound screwy to me I would have said that both Proctor and his sister were jealous of the attention the girl was paying a complete stranger. It was none of my business anyway.

But I didn't want to upset the Colonel or Mrs James; after all, they'd been helpful and they could probably help more if I was going to stay poking around in Fogel's business. I stood up abruptly.

'It's been very charming, Mrs James,' I said. 'But I've been imposing long enough. Thanks for your hospitality.'

Mrs James' face had cleared by now. Whatever psychological hang-ups she had were under control. She got up too and held out her hand.

'It has been nice,' she said. 'But like you said, it's a long drive. Henry will take you back to your own car.'

The girl put out her hand but she didn't say anything.

Mrs James leaned over and poured her another cup of tea as though she were the

housekeeper and the girl the owner of the house. Proctor was on his feet now, scraping back his chair. His face had cleared like the thing which had annoyed him had passed. As though to make amends he turned toward me with a broad smile which was more like his manner when we met an hour or two earlier.

'If I see anything else I'll give you a ring straight away, Mr Faraday.'

'That's kind, Colonel,' I said. 'I may come up again in a day or two in any event.'

Mrs James turned back toward me. She smiled a smile of great sweetness.

'In that case be sure to look in,' she said. 'Any time within reason. You'll always be welcome for a meal.'

'In fact you'd better make this your base,' Proctor said. 'It will be better than camping out at Place of Hawks.'

'That's very generous,' I said. 'I'll let you know.'

Mrs James waved as the Colonel and I walked over to the steps again. The sun was down now, throwing long shadows on the ground and the heat had lost a little of its bite. I looked back once. The girl was sitting looking after us, her hands folded in her lap. She didn't say anything or give any indication that she was conscious of our departure. Just before we got down the steps I saw Mrs James sit down close to her.

For a brief instant they looked like

something out of a Chekov play. Then I was following Proctor down the stone steps and the house was cut off.

The sun shimmered back off the Rolls' gleaming bodywork as we crunched over toward it. Proctor was silent, perspiration glistening on his red face and in among the roots of his hair.

'You seemed surprised at Caroline, Mr Faraday,' he said as he slid behind the wheel. He winced at the heat which came up from the leather cushions.

'I was expecting a housekeeper,' I said. 'She's a lovely girl.'

Proctor laughed. For once it had a harsh, unconvincing sound. I lowered myself into the passenger seat next to him, conscious of the searing heat which was biting through my clothing.

'She is that,' Proctor agreed, leaning forward to switch on. The engine was so quiet I had to listen hard for a moment to make sure it was going. Then Proctor smoothly engaged the gears and we glided forward down the slope. I glanced curiously at the Colonel. His manner had subtly changed since I'd arrived at the house. He looked like a crushed and chastened man.

'Is anything wrong?' I said.

Proctor shrugged.

'Nothing that a psychiatrist couldn't sort out,' he said shortly.

He spun the wheel, the power-steering taking the two-ton car effortlessly in the direction he wanted to go. The air was warmer now, as we came down off the hill. I could see the open gate of Place of Hawks steadily growing as the Rolls whispered round the steep curves toward the level of the main road that looped through the hills.

I lit a cigarette, put the spent match into the big dashboard tray. Proctor was smoking furiously, shovelling blue plumes of smoke over his shoulder, which the breeze ripped to tatters.

'Meaning what?' I said, in response to his remark of a minute earlier. I felt awkward, like I was prying into family secrets. But the girl Caroline had brought a strange atmosphere to the terrace up at the house. It was something half-hinted, like the echo of a piano playing somewhere in an old mansion. It was no business of mine and I didn't really want to get involved. But there was suddenly something rather pathetic about the strong figure of the Colonel.

He seemed to have shrivelled in the driving seat, his eyes screwed up as he gazed through the windscreen, like the smoke of his pipe was hurting his eyes. And he was determined to keep on throwing out fragments of information. I wondered what he expected me to say in return. I shot another glance at him as I feathered smoke out of my nostrils. There

was no apparent reaction to my question, so I guessed I hadn't said anything out of turn. He didn't say anything else until he'd tooled the big blue car into Place of Hawks. He drew up behind the Buick and switched off the motor. There was no sound now but the scuttering of birds in the bushes.

The green tunnel of trees pressing in on the driveway made a moist, damp passage that was somehow oppressive and menacing. Like Place of Hawks itself. So I sat and sweated and said nothing and waited for Proctor to go on. He sat with his big hands on the steering wheel. Something ran down his cheek and splashed on to his regimental tie. I got out the car and slammed the door. I hoped the diversion would give him time to get hold of himself.

'I brought her up here,' he said softly, more to himself than to me. 'She fell for Helen. My sister prefers the ladies. Funny how life works out.'

'You didn't have to tell me,' I said.

My words sounded awkward and banal, even to myself. The Colonel turned to face me. He was under control now.

'You'd have found out soon enough if you're coming up to the house again,' he said. 'They don't trouble to hide it. I thought I'd warn you.'

'I'm sorry,' I said.

The Colonel shook his head slowly. He sat there with his faded blue eyes staring like he

56

was searching for the key to something which had always eluded him.

'I got what I asked for,' he said slowly. 'No one's to blame. It's just life.'

He shook himself like a dog and became brisk and jovial again. He held out his big hand for me to shake.

'Nice to see you, Mr Faraday. We don't get many visitors. You'll always be welcome.'

He reversed the blue coupé and turned round. He didn't look back or wave. I stood and watched until the body of the car was lost among the trees.

CHAPTER SIX

1

I walked back down the driveway of Place of Hawks. There was no sound but the faint noises of birds. It was so clammy in here that I felt my shirt clinging to my back. Then the sun beat strongly on my face again as I came out the avenue and into the main concourse where the statue's face stared stonily at me over the waving grass. I looked at my wrist-watch. It was now around six and I ought to be moving soon.

But there were a couple of things more I wanted to do. I turned to look back and I

noticed something I hadn't seen before. There were a series of metal lamp posts, like something out of a movie depicting the nineteenth century, stretching down the driveway. They were painted green and when I had been driving up I obviously hadn't spotted them because they blended in with the foliage.

I remembered then that Fogel had said something about there being lights on the approach road. Apparently Proctor had driven along one evening to make sure. He hadn't mentioned anything about that. I wasn't sure now whether there had been two occasions or three when the lights were seen. Not that it was important. I walked along round the edge of the drive, my feet crunching hollowly in the silence of the late afternoon.

The Buick still sat with the sun burnishing the windshield. I figured the upholstery would be giving off about 120 degrees by now. I went back over to the porch and unlocked the front door, using the bunch of keys Fogel had given me. The house looked as Gothic and unreal as it had the moment I first set eyes on it. I padded through the ground floor rooms. Nothing appeared to have been disturbed. The kitchen door gave with a faint creaking noise.

I stood inside the door looking round carefully. There was a subtle difference in the room. I knew what it was then. The big old brass tap set over the stone sink was dripping again. I went over to it and tightened it

up. The dripping stopped. I frowned. I remembered distinctly turning off the tap not more than two hours before. I noticed something else then. The metal plates in the sink had disappeared.

While I was up at Proctor's place someone had come in and washed up. I grinned at the row of brown painted cupboards. 'House-proud ghosts,' I told the cooker.

I crossed over to the cupboards and opened up the door of the nearest. On the third shelf sat a set of metal plates. I touched one with my finger. There was just the faintest trace of dampness as I took my hand away. They were the plates which had contained scraps of food when I'd come in all right.

I shut the cupboard door and went back to the hall again. The rays of the setting sun were more yellow through the stained glass windows now. They'd soon be down beyond the rim of the hills. I switched off the electricity at the main and locked up. I went out to the Buick and tested the seat with my hand. It wasn't too bad now. I'd probably only get third degree burns. I eased behind the wheel, wincing as the heat seared through my jacket.

I started her up and eased the car along the drive to the stable area. The secondary road looped away from this and I followed it downhill, the Buick jolting round the bends over the uneven surface. I couldn't help contrasting it with Proctor's Rolls. You don't

live right, Mike, I told myself. The stream Fogel had spoken of cut across the road and through the meadows beyond.

It flowed into a small lake and was then lost in the far edge of the trees. There was a big old stone bridge straddling the water and I stopped the car on it for a moment, taking in the view. The stream chuckled to itself as it ran over boulders in the bed below and I wondered idly if there was any fishing there. Something else Fogel was missing out on. Something else too that didn't sit right.

I put the Buick in gear again and got off the bridge, following the road, still descending, between big shoulders of rock. I saw why visitors to Place of Hawks had to use the front entrance as I got round the next bend. There was a massive fallen tree across the roadway, completely blocking it. I stopped the Buick, killed the motor and got out. I walked up to the tree and then examined the banks at either side. There was no way I could get the Buick around, short of using a crane.

I lit a cigarette, flicking the spent match onto the roadway at my feet. I looked down beyond the tree to where the road snaked its way to a high wire gate. Beyond, there was nothing but hillside and more trees. The shadows were very full and black on the ground now. The tree had fallen from the bank, tearing its roots from the ground. The top had fallen on the bank beyond so that

there was about three feet clearance between the trunk and the road surface.

I squeezed underneath. I decided to walk down as far as the gate. I wondered if Fogel knew the road was blocked. Probably not or he would have mentioned it. I ducked under the tree and stood up. There was a low scarlet sport-car parked on the grass about five yards the other side of the tree. I went on over, treading quietly on the balls of my feet. There was no one in it. I bent over the steering wheel, trying to read the licence details strapped round the steering post.

There was a scraping noise and a voice said, 'Why don't you just ask? There's no secret.'

2

I straightened up, one hand resting on the steering wheel. The girl sitting up on top of the fallen tree, in a fork between two branches at the side of the road smiled.

'I hope I didn't frighten you,' she said.

'That's the second time someone's said that today,' I told her.

I walked back over and stood looking up at the girl. She was worth looking at. She was about twenty-eight to thirty years old, tall and with a lithe body that looked like she was used to exercise. It was a horseman's body without the tendency to seat that women riders get.

61

She had jet black hair that was so dark it was almost blue in shade. It was drawn back in a pony-tail and secured with a clip. She had a smooth, tanned face and level brown eyes that looked at me coolly and mockingly. Her nose was delicately moulded and tip-tilted. Her cheekbones were high and she had a wide, generous mouth that was ready to smile. She was smiling again now. Her teeth were perfect white ovals.

She had high, tight breasts that pressed forward ripely against the blue tailored shirt she was wearing. A brown leather belt with a big buckle enclosed a waist that my two hands could almost have spanned. Her stomach was absolutely flat and her long legs were encased in dark brown tailored slacks. She wore tan boots, highly polished and she dangled one leg lazily in the air, while her left was braced against a fork of the tree.

Her hands were small and well-cared for, without rings. She had a brown jacket lying by her side on the rough surface of the big branch on which she was sitting and there was a pack of cigarettes and a gold lighter lying on top of the jacket. She looked confident and sure of herself as she looked inquiringly down at me.

'You realize you're on private property?' she said at last.

Her voice was low and well-educated.

'I might say the same of you,' I said.

I walked up one of the sloping branches of

the big tree and sat down next to her. She looked at me gravely, as though weighing up my character. She tossed her head lightly, like she was irritated by the insects which were dancing a gavotte in the branches above us.

'I have a perfect right to be here,' she said.

She indicated the gate at the end of the road.

'I have a key. I often come up here.'

'Up here or to the house?' I said.

The girl shot me a questioning glance.

'What gives you the authority to ask me questions?' she said.

I shrugged.

'I've been engaged by the owner, Adelbert Fogel, to keep an eye on the place. I'm a private investigator from L.A. You can see my credentials if you like.'

'Don't bother,' the girl said calmly like she'd seen dozens of photostats in billfolds. She probably had, come to that. She looked at me some more, finally made up her mind. She held out her hand.

'I'm Samantha Fogel,' she said. 'Mr Fogel's my uncle.'

I took her hand. It was warm and strong. Her handshake was almost like a man's.

'He didn't say anything about you,' I said.

The girl crinkled up the corners of her mouth.

'He didn't say anything about you, Mr Faraday,' she returned. 'We're sort of in the

63

same boat, aren't we?'

'You could say that,' I said. 'What's your interest in Place of Hawks?'

The girl wriggled uneasily on the branch.

'I've known it since childhood,' she said. 'It's a favourite spot.'

She pointed back toward the gate again.

'I live about twenty miles down the road there. I sometimes come up for the afternoon and picnic and dream about the old days.'

'You get up to the house?' I said.

The girl looked at me sharply.

'Sometimes,' she said. 'Any special reason you should know?'

'Not really,' I said. 'Old man Fogel's a little worried about the security of the property. He asked me to have a looksee and made some recommendations.'

The girl wrinkled up her nose this time. It didn't make her look any less sensational.

'This your first day on the job?' she said.

'Sort of,' I said. 'I'd like to ask you some questions, Miss Fogel.'

'Fire away,' the girl said.

I shook my head.

'I haven't got time today. I've got to be making tracks toward L.A. But perhaps some other afternoon . . .'

'Be glad to,' the girl said. 'I'll give you my address and number. Give me a day's notice. Perhaps you'd like to come to the house for a meal.'

64

'I'll look forward to it,' I said.

I seemed to be getting no information on Fogel's assignment but plenty of social life. The girl was rummaging in the pocket of her jacket. She came up with a small pocket pad with a pencil stuck through a leather loop. She put the pad on her knee and scribbled furiously, the pink tip of her tongue just protruding from her mouth. She reminded me a little of the girl Caroline at that moment. Not much. This was a real woman.

I had a lot of questions I wanted to ask her. But like I said this wasn't the time. She gave me the slip of paper and I put it in my pocket.

'You wouldn't have a key of the house I suppose?' I said.

The girl looked at me steadily. There was no wavering of her direct gaze.

'There might be one at home,' she said. 'My father used to live here at one time, of course.'

'I didn't know,' I said.

'No reason why you should,' the girl said.

She slid off the bough with a rippling movement, picking up her things with her left hand and running down the branch to the ground almost as quickly as a squirrel. I guessed then that the tree had been down a long time. There was something of childhood in her familiarity with every knot and projection in the bark.

She stood by the sport-job and held out her hand.

'I must be going now,' she said. 'I've been up here for hours.'

'You haven't seen anyone else around?' I said.

The girl shook her head.

'Should I have?

'Just asking,' I said. 'If I'm checking on the place I'd better earn my fee.'

The girl grinned suddenly. She looked very young at that moment.

'Uncle Adelbert will make sure of it,' she said. 'I expect you've found that out already.'

'Anybody who uses string for shoelaces these days is either eccentric, on relief or a miser,' I said.

'Somewhere between one and three,' she said.

She slipped behind the wheel and revved up the engine. The little car started rolling over the turf and back down the track toward the far gate. I stood and watched it until the girl got out to open it. She waved again and I turned and ducked back under the tree. The sun was a long way down now and the air was already cooler but my shirt was still sticking to my back.

I got the Buick and jolted down the drive. I re-locked the gate of Place of Hawks behind me and lit a cigarette. The house belonging to Proctor sat on the hill opposite. It was full in the sun still, looking bland and innocent in the harsh light of early evening. Nothing moved on

66

the terrace now. I got back in the car. I had a lot to think about as I drove away.

CHAPTER SEVEN

1

It was around nine-thirty when I hit L.A. I decided to call in at the office in case Stella had left any messages. If I went home first I might have to go out again if there was anything urgent. I didn't expect there to be but you never know in my racket. I found a slot to park the Buick and walked a couple of blocks back. I rode up in the creaky elevator and opened up the door. I left it ajar and went on into the inner office and switched on the light. It had a curious atmosphere at night.

Something to do with the neons and the faint sound of traffic. But mostly the shadows I guess. They reminded me of all the people I'd known; all the cases where I'd failed; and all the characters I'd been unable to help. Even the bottle of bourbon in the desk drawer wasn't any good. Which was why I didn't stay around long nights. I switched on my own desk lamp and sat down in my swivel chair. The Smith-Wesson felt heavy so I unbuckled the holster and put it in the drawer.

There were a couple of messages from

Stella on my scratch-pad. Nothing urgent. One personal, both humorous. I sat smiling faintly to myself. I didn't sit there long. There was a grating noise on the linoleum of the waiting room and the door crashed back on its hinges. A character just slightly smaller than the Seagram Building stood framed in the lintel. I say framed advisedly. Another inch or two and he would have been embedded.

The giant came forward into the room. His shoulders would have made King Kong pause. He had hands like meat-hooks that hung low down at his sides. His dark brown suit must have been made out of Army surplus camouflage. His trousers were so baggy they looked like they were tailored out of old Zeppelins. He had a face like hammered sheet metal. His ears stood out like the handles on tea-cups. That was all I had time for. It would do to be going on with. I decided not to fool around with him.

'Your name Mike Faraday?' he said in a voice like a file going through a cell-bar. With that soundbox he couldn't have played Jane Austen in summer stock. I guessed it wouldn't have worried him much.

'That's what it says on the door,' I said. 'Come in and rest your feet.'

'I ain't got time for games,' he said. 'Daddy Pushkin don't want you poking around Wuthering Heights.'

'Daddy Pushkin can go milk a duck,' I said.

68

King Kong made a clicking noise. He shook his head and looked at me reproachfully. He leaned forward and took hold of my shoulder thoughtfully. His hand felt like a steel claw. He lifted me from the desk and held me in the air. All the while he looked at me with sad eyes in his battered face. Then he let me go. I thought I was going to go right through the seat of the chair. The impact must have been heard way down on the ground floor.

'I'm going to get annoyed in a minute,' I said.

The big ape gurgled with amusement. He reached out again and took hold of my shoulder.

'Try the other one,' I said. 'Then I got the set.'

I waited while he digested this. He was so strong he could have thrown my suit from here to Ocean Beach. With me in it.

'Daddy Pushkin wouldn't like your attitude,' he said.

'You know what you can tell Daddy Pushkin,' I said.

The giant shrugged.

'You'd better come tell him yourself,' he said.

I tried to wriggle out the big man's grasp, only made my shoulder throb more painfully.

'What's the alternative?' I said.

The big ape shrugged again.

'You get dead,' he said.

'All the way?' I said.

'All the way,' the big man said.

'I wouldn't like that,' I said.

The big man let go my shoulder and stepped away from the desk. He stood watching me thoughtfully, then turned toward the door. I sat back in my chair, massaging my suit into position. I felt like I'd been run over by a bulldozer. King Kong was standing by the door now.

'You coming?' he said.

I got up. 'I'm coming,' I told him.

2

I switched off my desk-lamp and walked on over to him. He waited until I got up close and then grabbed my shoulder again. He ran over me like it was an afterthought. I was glad I wasn't carrying the Smith Wesson now.

'I'm clean,' I said.

The big man grunted.

'You expect me to take your word for it?'

'You can take my word,' I said. 'If I'd had a gun I'd have stopped you before now.'

The big man stepped back from me and grunted again. His hammered metal face expressed surprise. Then he gave a broad grin. Up closer he wasn't without humour. He let go my shoulder. I switched off the lights and we went out in the corridor. He waited while I

locked up. The elevator wasn't working now so we walked down.

'Your car or mine?' I said.

'We'll take mine,' the big man said. 'I'll bring you back to pick up your heap.'

'I'm coming back then?' I said.

'If you behave,' Kong said.

We walked half a block to where a big black Cadillac sat. I got in the passenger seat and the big man slammed the door after me. He went around to the driving seat.

Now that I had time to study him I noticed for the first time that he had almost black eyes. They were like splintered glass in which little flickers of something surfaced from time to time. Though what I couldn't say. I was never able to read the expression in them. When they seemed at rest the big man might be most likely to do something violent. He had crinkled hair that looked almost negroid, the way it clustered round his skull.

It was greying at the edges. I put his age at around fifty but he was in very hard condition; he had all the ear-marks of an ex-pug who kept in training. Or perhaps a pro-wrestler who still worked out once in a while. I knew I wouldn't stand any chance against him. A cop materialised from the shadows while Kong was wrapping himself around the wheel. He was a mild-looking young man with steel-rimmed glasses. He cleared his throat like he was nervous.

'You know you're parked in front of a fire-plug?' he said to the big man.

The ape glowered.

'Breeze off,' he told the cop briskly.

The mild man coloured and looked at me as though for moral support. I kept on gazing frontwards. I didn't want to be wearing my head the wrong way round. The cop swallowed once or twice and tried again. He moved around to the driver's door and started to open it. Kong got ponderously out the driving seat. He just seemed to keep on going. The mild cop gulped and the whites of his eyes showed. He made a strangled noise low down in his throat. He put his hand down toward the holster of his revolver. The big man sighed.

'You heard what I said,' he told a passing street car.

He reached down and tore the cop's leather belt in half like I take the wrapping off a package of cigarettes. He hurled the belt and revolver over on to the sidewalk. There was a moment's silence and then the tinkle of breaking glass.

'Yes, sir,' the cop said in a strangled voice.

He walked off in the direction the revolver had gone, trying to look casual. He was making a very poor job of it. Kong eased himself behind the wheel again. He bellowed with sudden gusts of laughter.

'Did you see his face?' he said. 'Christ, what a crowd of creeps . . .'

I didn't say anything. It didn't seem the time. The big man suddenly turned toward me. He came up with a red silk handkerchief that was about as big as the bath towels they supply at the Hilton. He folded it several times until he had it in the shape of a flat bandage.

'I got to blindfold you, Mr Faraday,' he said. 'Instructions.'

'Sure,' I said. 'We wouldn't want to upset Daddy Pushkin.'

'You ain't seen Daddy Pushkin,' the giant said seriously.

'He must be something if he worries you,' I said.

King Kong grunted.

'Nothing worries me,' he said. 'But when Daddy Pushkin says something everybody takes notice.'

He bound the handkerchief over my eyes; it was so big it went round my head twice. My eyelids felt gummed to my cheeks and the stink of whisky and tobacco was in my nostrils. The big man tied the knot so tight I felt a momentary roaring in my ears. Then he relaxed and took his hand away.

'This won't take long,' he said.

He started the motor and gunned the big car out from the sidewalk. I couldn't hear any police whistles so I guessed the mild-looking cop had decided to get out with only a broken belt. He was ahead of the game at that. The car travelled straight for a few hundred yards

and then turned sharp left.

I sat back on my seat and held the door-handle with my right hand, listening to the slurring of the tyres on hot tarmac and counting the turns and intersections. I needn't have wasted my time. Before we'd travelled a mile the big man had made so many turns and swerving movements that I was completely lost. Traffic noises didn't help much either; they don't in a city. The big man chuckled. He drove well and fast and after a few minutes more of obvious horsing around he straightened up and put his toe down. Other than that we were somewhere in L.A. I hadn't got a clue. I took my hand away from the door-handle and turned toward the driver.

'Mind if I smoke?' I said.

'Go ahead,' the big man said.

I got out my package and put a cigarette in my mouth. I heard a matchhead flare beside me. It sounded like Kong was striking it on his thumb. He put the light to the tip of the cigarette as I puffed.

'You got a monicker or are you incognito?' I said.

'Not on these sort of jobs,' the big man said. 'Only among my friends.'

The conversation died after that. We'd been travelling about forty minutes when I felt the car slacken, the driver applied the brakes and then we were turning again. The Caddy's springing gave softly as we rumbled over some

sort of ramp and then the engine was idling back and we seemed to be between high walls. The tyres crunched again and we came to a halt. Kong killed the motor. I could feel a hot wind blowing from somewhere and with it the sickly smells of cooking. Probably from a grating.

'You get out here,' the pug said in his rusty-tin voice. 'Don't try anything.'

I got out and closed the door of the Caddy behind me. I could hear the big man's feet coming toward me. He untied the bandage and pushed me forward. I had just time to see we were in a narrow alley between high walls. There were rows of trash bins ranged against the opposite wall and stacks of cardboard cartons on the other side.

We went in a pair of swing doors painted black and started walking down a cement corridor. A blast of cool air came out of trunking set in the ceiling. We went on down the passage toward another set of double doors at the other end.

CHAPTER EIGHT

1

A grey carpet stretched on ahead as we got through the entrance. There were walnut

doors set at intervals either side and in the far distance I could hear a band playing. From the cooking smells, the layout and the music we might be in some sort of club. It didn't help much. There were hundreds to choose from.

The man mountain didn't say anything but I could hear him keeping pace with me about two steps behind. His weight made the corridor tremble. We kept on going. I turned right at his grunted direction when we got to the end of the corridor. We went up a narrow stairway with a wrought iron railing. There was another walnut door up ahead facing the stairs. It had Private painted on it in gold curlicue script. We went on through.

We were in a big office with panelled walls. Desk lamps burned on antique bureaux. There were sporting prints on the walls and the pile of the carpet was so thick it caught me behind the knees. I waited while the big man locked the door behind me. There was no one in the room. The ape passed me and went on down the far end to where there was another closed door.

'Wait here,' he called over his shoulder.

'You mean I got a choice?' I said.

He didn't answer that. I waited until he'd tapped on the door and gone inside. I went over and tried the handle of the door behind me. Like I figured it was locked. I wandered around the room. The windows all faced the blank wall of the alley opposite so they didn't

tell me anything. There was nothing on the bureaux and no phone in the room. I stood there for about five minutes looking at the heavy marble fireplace and the sporting prints and thinking about nothing.

The far door opened and the big man's shoulders backed out. He stood holding the door ajar and beckoned to me. I could hear the murmur of a voice from inside the room.

I heard someone say, 'We can handle it,' as I got up level with the doorway. The big man stood aside and waited until I'd passed him. I heard the key turn in the door lock.

This was a smaller office than the first. Heavy drapes reached from floor to ceiling on one side. That facing the alley I guessed. The door was padded with red leather I saw as I glanced at the big ape in rear. No sound from the outside penetrated here. The walls were wood panelled too and the carpet was even thicker than in the room we'd left. The light came from three or four heavy table lamps with parchment shades that were set on low tables around the room.

There was a bar up one end with white leather stools set along it like the owner of the office was used to entertaining. The man who was just putting down the ivory telephone as we came in got up and stood behind his massive desk.

'I must apologise for this unorthodox method of requesting an interview, Mr

Faraday,' he said with a bland smile. He waved me to a chair in front of the desk and I sank down into the deep tan leather. The big man stood behind me and breathed heavily.

'Requesting?' I said.

The man standing behind the desk laughed politely.

'Sam is a little overpowering isn't he?'

He moved easily and reseated himself in his black leather swivel chair. He folded two well manicured hands together on the blotter and looked at me shrewdly.

'We'll just have to efface any false impression, my dear sir.'

He jerked his head toward the bar in rear.

'First a drink. Then we talk. Name your poison.'

We both sat and studied each other while Sam shambled over to the bar and started fooling around with glasses and stirring rods. Pushkin was a man of about fifty-five with one of those vaguely Central European faces that don't stamp themselves very vividly on one's consciousness. Fleshy lips, well groomed hair, silver-grey and fashionably curling over his ears; black eyebrows, strong white teeth; slim, artistic hands.

He wore an expensive-looking gold wristlet watch and he was smoking a Turkish cigarette through a green jade holder with gold bands. His voice was low and well educated but with a strong European accent. He wore full evening

dress; white tie and tails, so I guessed this was some sort of night spot. These sort of characters didn't usually dress for dinner in a private house and he had gambling club proprietor stamped all over him. I didn't take to him very much.

Kong was back now; he put the long glass in my hand. Pushkin hadn't asked me what I wanted. It was bourbon with plenty of ice. I tasted it. It was all right. Pushkin sat behind his desk and watched me with deep brown eyes which were quite expressionless. He waited until Sam had put the tall glass full of greenish liquid on the blotter at his elbow before he spoke again.

'I figured you for a bourbon man, Mr Faraday,' he said with satisfaction.

'You were right,' I said.

'Mr Pushkin's hardly ever wrong,' Sam said in his rusted-tin voice.

Pushkin closed his hands round the tall glass with a convulsive movement like he was going to crush it. His eyes looked venom at the big man over my shoulder.

'Fool!'

His voice cracked like a whip.

'Why don't you give him my address as well while you're at it.'

I half-swivelled in my chair and glanced at the big man. The change in him was remarkable. There was almost a cringing look on his face as he shuffled his feet like a three-

year-old child caught stealing the cream off the milk.

'Sorry, Mr Pushkin,' he said. 'I didn't think.'

The club owner had recovered himself by now. He put his hands together on the blotter in front of him and studied his immaculate fingernails intently.

'That's your trouble, Sam,' he said in a tired voice. 'Wait outside. I'll call you if I need you.'

Pushkin waited until the door had closed softly behind the giant. He gave me a bleak smile.

'The help one is forced to rely on nowadays . . .'

He broke off and waved an expansive finger.

'But I'm forgetting my manners, Mr Faraday. A cigar?'

He indicated a silver box on the corner of the desk. I shook my head.

'Never use them. I'll smoke my own if you don't mind.'

Pushkin leaned back in his chair and pulled his glass closer toward him. He sat with it cradled in his lap. His eyes were focused somewhere up on the corner of the ceiling now. I got out my pack and lit up. I put the spent match stalk back in the box and replaced it in my pocket. I focused up on Pushkin again through the smoke. He tried a half-smile, found it didn't work.

'Where was I, Mr Faraday?'

'You were complaining about the quality of

80

the help,' I said.

Pushkin shook his head and half-closed his eyes. He looked like a man in whom impatience always simmered just below the surface. He hadn't shown his strength yet. But he must have had a lot of personality to have put the giant Sam down so effectively. He was operating in low gear so far as I was concerned. I decided to wait and see what he wanted. There was no sense in antagonizing him too early. In the event he ignored my remark. He opened his eyes again.

'I trust your drink is to your satisfaction, Mr Faraday?'

'Just fine,' I said. 'But I'd still like to know why you brought me here.'

'All in good time,' Pushkin said.

He got up suddenly and eased back his chair. He went over to the far side of the big room and did something to the panelling. A door opened in it. There was the usual safe behind it. I wondered when the guys who operated gambling clubs would come up with something really original. Pushkin was shielding the safe with his back as he dialled the combination.

He finished at last and grunted with satisfaction. He closed up the safe, put back the panelling and came over to his desk again. He slid a long buff envelope over toward me. I leaned forward and picked it up. The contents crackled. I knew what was in it before I

opened the envelope. There was a big bundle of notes in there. They still had the denomination band on from the bank.

Pushkin watched me with narrowed eyes.

'There's ten thousand dollars there, Mr Faraday,' he said softly. 'Go on and count it.'

I put the envelope back on the desk.

'I'll take your word for it, Mr Pushkin,' I said. 'Very nice indeed. Just what do I have to do for it?'

Pushkin chuckled softly.

'Nothing,' he said.

2

'I don't get you,' I said.

Pushkin swivelled in his chair.

'Come, Mr Faraday,' he said. 'You're a sensible man. I've heard about you around town now for quite a few years. You've always impressed me as a man who could figure the angles right.'

I swirled my drink in the glass, admiring the colour against the shaded lamps.

'You heard right, Mr Pushkin,' I said.

Pushkin chuckled. He drew his fleshy lips back over his gums so that he reminded me of some well-fed zoo animal. A dangerous animal at that. I didn't underestimate him.

'So that we can regard it as settled, Mr Faraday?'

'Regard what as settled?' I said.

Pushkin expelled the breath from his mouth in an expressive gesture of annoyance.

'For a smart private eye you're proving remarkably obtuse, Mr Faraday.'

I lifted my glass to my mouth again before replying.

'Suppose you enlighten me.'

Pushkin's brown eyes flickered. He seemed inordinately interested in the green liquid in the long glass on his blotter.

'I'm trying to be discreet, Mr Faraday,' he said. 'I don't want to have to spell it out.'

'You're going to have to if we're going to do business,' I said.

I looked again at the big bundle of notes in the envelope.

'You send your gorilla to pick me up and then you offer me ten thousand dollars for nothing. That's a lot of money for a zero result.'

Pushkin pursed his lips and looked at me shrewdly.

'That's exactly what the deal is. That's how I'd like to keep it. I know you but you don't know me. You walk out that door with the money and that's the end of the matter.'

'Except I know your name,' I said. 'It wouldn't take me long to trace this place. Some sort of club, isn't it?'

Pushkin turned his brown eyes on me levelly. There was a hard quality in them which

hadn't been there before.

'You wouldn't find that very profitable, Mr Faraday,' he said. 'Believe me.'

'Place of Hawks,' I said. 'You're interested in Place of Hawks.'

Pushkin picked up his glass again and sipped fastidiously at the green liquid. With his distinguished air and the evening dress he looked more like Otto Kruger than ever.

'You have the point precisely,' he said. 'Your activities there are unwelcome to a client of mine.'

'You wouldn't care to be more specific?' I said.

Pushkin shook his head.

'I can't afford to be, Mr Faraday. Let's just say that you're being given a lot of money to drop the case. Beyond that I can't and won't go. You must admit it's a pretty generous fee for the work involved.'

He had a point there. I put down my glass on the desk in front of me.

'Supposing I don't accept the offer?'

Pushkin's eyes narrowed. He ran a slender finger round the rim of his glass.

'I'm sure you wouldn't do anything so foolish, Mr Faraday.'

'What about my client?' I said.

Pushkin shrugged. His brown eyes were snake-like as he watched me without blinking.

'That's your business, Mr Faraday. I leave it to you. No doubt it wouldn't be the first time

84

where a case didn't pan out.'

'I don't operate like that,' I said.

Pushkin's eyebrows shot up.

'Meaning what?'

'Meaning that I'm not interested,' I said. 'You can keep your money.'

I stood up. Pushkin smiled a frozen smile.

'If that's all we've got to talk about I'll be on my way,' I said.

Pushkin shook his head.

'You're being extremely foolish, Mr Faraday,' he said. 'You'd better take the money.'

He leaned forward and pushed the envelope containing the bills back toward me.

'What I'd like to know is why you're so interested in Place of Hawks,' I said.

The club proprietor's distinguished-looking head swivelled toward me. There was genuine admiration in his eyes.

'You're a remarkable man, Mr Faraday,' he said. 'Just exactly how do you think you're going to get out?'

'I'll think of something,' I said.

I went over the desk in a long, shallow dive. I got to Pushkin's hand before it touched the buzzer. He gave a strangled yelp and his chair went over backward. We landed on the floor in a tangle of arms and legs. I hoped the music outside would cover the noise we were making. Pushkin gave a high shriek like a woman as I slapped him three times across the face. Saliva

ran out the corner of his mouth. The small nickel-plated revolver fell from his trembling fingers and rolled across the carpet. There were angry red weals running over his cheek now.

The chair came over on top of us and then I had twisted aside. My hand closed over the gun and I got up. One of Pushkin's flailing feet caught me around the ankles and almost brought me down again. The pain stung me for a moment and I reached out and grabbed him by the hair. Tears of agony came into his eyes and rolled down toward the corners of his mouth. I threw the safety-catch of the toy pistol and put it up close to his ear.

'Any more noise, sonny and this goes off,' I said. 'Understand?'

Pushkin gave a strangled grunt low in his throat. He looked a pitiful object with his ruffled hair and watery eyes. They were a dull muddy colour now.

'I'll kill you for this,' he mumbled.

'It's been tried before,' I said. 'Now we'll just walk out of here nice and slow and if King Kong tries to interfere you'll be the first to get it.'

Pushkin swallowed once or twice. I let go his hair and he slumped backward and would have fallen if I hadn't caught his shoulder. I got his chair and hauled it upright, pushed him into it.

'We'd better understand one or two things before I go out of here,' I said. 'Firstly, I can't

be bought. Secondly, I don't push around. And thirdly, I'm asking the questions.'

Pushkin smoothed down his hair and put a trembling hand up to his cheek. With his yellow face and blazing eyes he looked like a mediaeval picture of death. He fought to get control of his voice for a minute or two.

'That's the first time I've been involved in physical violence for over twenty years,' he said. 'The last two people who tried it died—slowly.'

'You'd better make mine thirty or forty years,' I said. 'The longer the better. I asked you about Place of Hawks just now. You'd better come up with some quick answers. I have a nasty temper.'

Pushkin smiled a twisted smile. He was recovering himself now. His eyes roamed round the room with quick, flickering glances.

'You won't have time even for quick answers, Mr Faraday,' he said. 'Just how do you think you're going to get out of here. Have you forgotten Sam?'

He had a point.

'We'll continue this some place else,' I said. 'Just remember what I said.'

I waved the toy pistol in front of his face.

'Any interference and this goes off.'

Some of the yellow was back in Pushkin's face now. He licked his lips with a bluish tongue. He got up and smoothed his rumpled tail-suit. He shrugged.

I moved around behind him as he got out from behind the desk. He walked in front of me toward the door. I jammed the pistol in against his spine.

'Open the door nice and easy,' I told him. 'If Sam's there tell him to step aside.'

'Sam won't be there,' Pushkin said. 'He'll have gone across the corridor. There's a private bar there. I ring for him if I want him.'

He opened the door. I stared over his shoulder. The panelled room was empty. There was one big shaded lamp burning in the corner. I closed Pushkin's office door behind me and prodded him forward toward the door that led to the corridor. We were about three-quarters of the way there when something stirred in the shadows. The curtains billowed in the hot wind from outside. I shifted the pistol up, a fraction too late. I saw Kong's face just before a ten-ton truck fell on me. Then I passed out.

CHAPTER NINE

1

Something ran down my face, dripped off my chin. I heard a groaning noise. It was originating from me. Pushkin's face was coming into focus now. He had a crooked

smile pasted on his distinguished features. I shifted my head, felt a blinding pain in my neck. Sam's giant form moved ponderously, as he eased his position on the desk. He clicked his teeth.

'I told you to take it easy, pal,' he said sorrowfully.

'I never follow other people's advice,' I told him.

Somebody hit me across the mouth. The blow stung but it was what I needed to wake me up. The fog cleared from my eyes. There was a third man at my side. He was big and had a lumpy white face. The light in the room glistened on his oiled black hair. He adjusted the glove on his right fist and grunted. He looked questioningly at Pushkin. I noticed there were black stains on the glove.

'We were discussing my offer before the unfortunate violence began,' Pushkin said. 'It still stands.'

I shook my head.

'It's the small print on my contract,' I said. 'It says something about keeping faith with the clients.'

'You're being very foolish,' Pushkin said. 'However, I must admit, while admiring your integrity I am not averse to a little more violence—on your person, of course.'

He smirked and dabbed his cheek with a lace handkerchief.

'Of course,' I said.

My head snapped back as the man with the oiled hair slapped me again. He seemed to enjoy his work. There was a light of enthusiasm in his eyes. He hit me several times more. I must have passed out. When I came around there was a dull throbbing in my jaws. Big Sam had my face in his two hands. He was looking down at me almost tenderly.

'Don't cut him up too much,' he said in a low voice.

The man with the oiled hair grunted something. Water trickled down my face. I kept my eyes closed and sagged forward in the chair like I was worse beat up than I was. I wasn't faking very much though. I'd been out twice and my head was so muzzy I couldn't tell whether that was the total or whether I'd been out before that.

My head felt like a balloon and midgets with trimming bars were playing a gavotte on my skull that must have been heard the other side of town. The big man moved away. I felt rather than heard him go. I instinctively braced myself for another session with the gloves but nothing happened for a minute or two. Then I felt my chin raised by sharp fingers. I opened my eyes. Pushkin's eyes looked into my own. There was a lot of satisfaction in his glance.

'We'll put the money in your pocket when we've finished,' he said. 'Just in case you change your mind.'

'I shan't change my mind,' I said.

90

I jerked my head up. Pushkin moved just too late. I felt my skull connect with his chin with a satisfying crack. Pushkin gave a howl of pain as he went over backwards. I heard him crash into the desk. The man with dark oiled hair came back like a panther and snapped my head back with the glove. I tasted blood.

Then he went over to join Big Sam. He was behind the desk helping Pushkin up. I opened my eyes. Pushkin looked a mess. Blood was trickling in a thin stream down his chin. His face was chalk white and he pushed furiously away from the big man's restraining hand. He got the handkerchief and clapped it over his mouth. He looked like a dentist's patient as he tottered up toward me.

'There are some people who won't be taught,' he mumbled. 'I've finished with you.'

'Is that definite?' I said. 'Because if so it's worth looking forward to.'

'You won't be so humorous when we've finished,' Pushkin said.

His hand came up holding the little automatic. He whirled it above his head. It came down in a shining arc. I closed my eyes, heard a stunning crack. I felt no pain. I opened my eyes again. Big Sam's hand had taken the smack. He held Pushkin's arm immovable.

'You ain't yourself, boss,' he said in his harsh voice. 'You'll think better of it in a minute.'

He put the club owner's arm gently down

again. Pushkin stood for a moment, his face a crumpled mask of pain. Then he smiled wryly. He looked affectionately at the battered face of the giant.

'You are not often right, Sam,' he said gently. 'But on this occasion I think you have a point. And it would be inartistic as well as pointless to kill him at this stage.'

He adjusted his jacket and went over to look at his face in a wall mirror. He came back again, dabbing tenderly at his cut chin. He looked at me without saying anything for a moment or two more.

'After all,' he said, more to himself than to the others, 'what do I employ muscle for?'

He nodded to the man with the oiled hair. He came in swinging again. I only felt the first two blows. I counted more fireworks and then I passed out. This time I took longer to come around. I became aware of lights and blurred shapes. The shapes translated themselves into the face of Big Sam and the figure of Pushkin. I found my hands were untied. I flexed my fingers and tried to struggle up in the chair. The giant gently pushed me back.

'Take it easy, pal,' he said. 'You ain't ready for that yet.'

I was back in the chair in front of Pushkin's desk. He sat behind it looking like his old unruffled self. Apart from the cut on his chin and a slight paleness of the face he might have passed for normal. Except for the ferocity

which shone out of his eyes whenever he turned toward me.

'Can you hear me, Faraday?' he said.

A croaking noise came out my mouth. I didn't recognize myself. I nodded, stopped because of the blinding pain in my neck. My jaws were throbbing and lights were dancing in the darkness of my brainbox. Leastways, that's what it seemed like. I could feel my shirt sticking damply to my chest. That would be when they'd thrown the water to revive me. I could feel caked blood on the side of my head now. I opened my eyes, forced the room into focus. There was no sign of the man with the oiled hair and the gloves. I hoped I'd meet him again when the odds were more level.

Pushkin leaned forward and put his elbows on the desk. A blue cloud of Turkish cigarette smoke hung in the air above him. He had the green jade holder with gold bands back in his mouth again. His deep brown eyes were steady and under control now.

'I hope I make myself clear,' he said. 'This is your only warning. You chose to repudiate the handsome present I offered you. I've told you to lay off the case. If you choose to go on you have only yourself to blame.'

I tried to come up with a crack, found I couldn't articulate anything. My mouth and lips seemed to be swollen. The man with the gloves had certainly given me a going-over. He probably worked on me while I was out.

'I guess he got the message, boss,' Big Sam said. He looked almost solicitous as he hovered over me.

'Let's hope so, Sam,' Pushkin said.

He stood up and put the envelope and the bundle of bills back in his pocket. My eyes were focusing properly now so I guessed they weren't damaged. Pushkin stood behind the desk looking down sombrely at me.

'You'd best get him back to where you found him,' he told the big man. 'We've wasted enough time on this farce tonight.'

'Sure, boss,' the giant said. 'You won't have any more trouble.'

He picked me up like I was no more weight than a rag doll. He seemed anxious to get out before Pushkin changed his mind. I stood the jolting as Sam pounded across the floor toward the door. Then I must have passed out for the count.

2

I felt someone shaking my shoulder. I picked up what was left of my face and squinted up in the direction of the voice. I'd been leaning on the dashboard of a car and I felt like the controls were stencilled on my forehead. I was back in the Buick. It was still parked a couple of blocks from my office so I figured Sam must have been tailing me when I hit L.A. That

94

might be worth looking into. Right now I had other things to think about.

'You drunk, buddy, or what?'

I stared. My eyelids were ungummed and some of the headache was going away. It was the mild-looking cop with glasses Big Sam had busted earlier on. His eyes opened wide and a hissing noise came out his mouth as he took in my face.

'Jesus Christ, buddy,' he said mildly. 'You been hit by a beer-truck or what?'

I cleared my throat, found I could talk.

'Just about,' I said in a harsh voice. 'The big guy who tore up your gunbelt. Remember?'

The cop turned pink.

'As if I could forget,' he said. 'You want to prefer charges?'

'Do you?' I said.

The mild-looking cop took his eyes off my own, focused on the pavement at his feet.

'I see what you mean,' he said.

I struggled up in my seat and looked at myself in the driving mirror. I didn't like what I saw. I took my eyes off the mirror.

'Providing you could find him,' I said.

'I ought to get some sort of report out,' the cop said helplessly.

'That's up to you,' I said. 'His name's Sam if that helps any. My name's Faraday. I'm a private investigator with offices in the building where he assaulted you. That's about all I know. Some muscle sent around by someone

who doesn't like my operations, probably. It happens every day.'

The cop had his notebook out by now. He looked at it dubiously, shut it up and put his pencil away.

'You think I'm wasting my time, then?'

I nodded.

'It might happen to you every day,' the mild cop said. He shuddered suddenly and looked at me with awe.

'I'm a traffic clerk normally. They got some of us out of the office because of a shortage of personnel.'

I started the motor of the Buick and listened to its idling above the faint roar of the boulevard traffic.

'Take my advice and get back inside,' I told him. 'You'll find it a lot safer.'

I gunned off out before he could come up with a reply. The rush of air was clearing my head. I took it nice and slow and got over to my Park West house without actually crashing into any other vehicles. I got a few horn concertos though. I put the Buick in the car-port and found my keys. It took me three or four minutes to get the door open. I was still thinking about switching on the light when I went down again.

When I woke I felt a whole lot better. I struggled up and put on a shaded lamp in the living room. If my wrist watch hadn't stopped it was after three a.m. I got undressed and

dragged myself upstairs. All the weight of the world seemed to be on my shoulders. But there were no bones broken anywhere. The dark-haired boy had made sure of that.

I got under a hot shower and rotated in the needle spray of the water. I wrapped a big towel around me and padded down to the kitchen. I had three cups of scalding hot coffee and grabbed a sandwich. It was around four when I went back up to the bedroom. I grabbed an automatic from the small armoury I keep in a locked cupboard there. I put it under my pillow. I didn't go anywhere near a mirror. I knew what I looked like and there would be time enough for that tomorrow. I was asleep almost as soon as I lowered myself on to the pillow.

CHAPTER TEN

1

It was around ten when I hit Adelbert Fogel's place. To my surprise I felt almost back to normal. My face was still throbbing and there was a bruise on my temple. For the rest there was a redness and a feel of sand-paper along my cheeks which might almost have come from sun and wind. In fact the jazzy blonde number I was surprised to find in the outer

oak reception room of Fogel's office had put her own interpretation on it.

She grinned when I showed up at the railed-in enclosure where she was buffing her nails in between sessions of pecking at her typewriter. She put her head on one side and gave me a cool look.

'Don't tell me,' she said. 'You went sailing over the week-end and forgot to duck when the boom came over.'

'How did you guess?' I said.

The blonde number grinned again.

'My steady's a sailing buff,' she said. 'We go over to Santa Monica some week-ends.'

'That's quite a drive,' I said.

The blonde shook her head and squinted at her immaculate nails.

'Not the way my steady drives,' she said. 'You wanted to see somebody?'

'I might as well while I'm here,' I said.

Just then one of the oak doors in rear opened and a man came out. He was young and snappily dressed in a bright blue suit. He had on a shirt which looked like a pair of pyjamas and a jazzy silk tie to match. I blinked. I hadn't expected such visions in old Fogel's chambers. He was about thirty and he had dark black hair that was parted almost symmetrically in the middle. He had carefully tended sidepieces and a tanned, strong face.

There was something about the mouth that seemed vaguely familiar. He had strong white

teeth and grey eyes and he walked with a quick, springy stride that made me think of something not at all connected with lawyer's offices. He paused and gave me a sharp look, while he fumbled with a brown card folder he was holding.

'I'd like to see Mr Adelbert Fogel,' I told the girl.

I spoke deliberately loudly so that the Rhapsody in Blue could hear me properly. He gave a slight start but he didn't say anything. The blonde job had half-swivelled in her chair to look at him over her shoulder but now she turned back to me again.

'I don't know about that,' she said, with a faint frown. 'He's awful busy today.'

'He'll see me all right,' I said. 'Just give him my card.'

I rummaged around in my wallet as the sharp character in blue came over.

'Mr Fogel doesn't see anybody without an appointment,' he said in a cutting manner.

I grinned. The girl was examining my business card. Her manner had subtly changed.

'Would you mind asking him?' I said.

The dark man shrugged.

'It wouldn't do any good,' he said discouragingly.

'I don't think you quite understand,' I said. 'Mr Fogel's engaged my services. He'll be available any time of day or night.'

The dark man didn't quite jump but he almost managed it. A startled expression passed across his face and he bit his lip.

'I think you'd better listen to this gentleman, Alex,' the blonde job said. She passed the card over. The young man took it and studied it for a moment. Another remarkable change passed across his features.

'Mr Faraday's a sailing buff too,' the girl said brightly.

'I think it would be best if you kept out of this, Dilys,' the dark man said crisply.

He smiled suddenly and held out his hand.

'I'm Alex Fogel,' he said. 'My father's the principal here. Sorry about the mix-up. You didn't make yourself clear at the beginning.'

I took his hand. He opened the gate in the enclosure and waved me through.

'That's all right,' I said. 'I'm used to it. Though I didn't expect to find this set-up.'

Fogel smiled. He looked around the office and back to the girl approvingly. The way she looked at him I didn't have to guess twice who her sailing companion was.

'This is for the customers,' Fogel said. 'You've met my father?'

I nodded.

'Wait until you see his own office,' Fogel said. 'That's something again.'

'Different is it?' I said.

'Different,' Fogel said.

He gave a low whistle, way down in his

throat.

'Dombey and Son. When father goes we're going to ship the whole lot straight to the Museum.'

He motioned to me to wait where I was and went off through a door in back. I studied a calendar that advertised a mortician's day and night service and promised the satisfied client a long sleep amid the pines, before turning to the more rewarding back of the blonde job. She certainly had everything it took and more.

I was still admiring the coachwork when Fogel was at my elbow again.

'Go right in, Mr Faraday,' he said. 'Dad tells me it's confidential so I won't come in.'

'You mean to say you don't know my business with your father?' I said.

Fogel shook his head. His eyes were focused over my shoulder at the figure of Dilys in the background. I guessed I might have interrupted something when I came in.

'Dad keeps his life in different compartments,' he said. 'Is there any reason I shouldn't know your business?'

'None at all,' I said. 'Except I gave your father my word. I guess he'll tell you if he figures it's necessary.'

Fogel nodded. There was a slightly baffled expression on his face. I left him standing there and went over to the oak door which had Fogel's name on it in gold leaf script. The door was slightly ajar so I didn't need to knock so

loudly. I walked on in and closed the door behind me in response to the old man's bleating invitation to enter. I blinked. Fogel Jr. certainly hadn't exaggerated.

2

The room was a big one but it seemed microscopic because of the vast amount of junk in it. There were papers stacked in bundles in chairs, on the floor, on desks, on shelves set along the wall and on the top of cupboards. It took me some time to locate old man Fogel there was so much stuff. The dust was so thick on everything it seemed to hover tangibly in the air. My footsteps raised a thin carpet of dust as I walked, threading my way between the papers, and there was a pallid imprint of my feet on the flooring behind me.

There were no lights burning. There wouldn't be, of course. That would be against my client's notion of economy. What light there was came through two big windows in back; made of greenish tinted glass they gave one's face a decayed tinge. All the while I was there old man Fogel was giving a pretty good imitation of a corpse. As his face was cadaverous to start with the impression was startling.

The name of the firm was painted on the windows and re-echoed on the floor at my feet

by the California sunshine which was doing its best to break through the coating of dust on the glass. It was just about holding its own. Despite the heat the windows were closed and there were no fans going. I guessed that was because of the high risk of choking in this atmosphere. Fogel had a desk by the window and it took me a moment or two more to place him.

The sheer bulk of wastepaper on the desk made a sort of rampart round the old boy. I caught a movement and there was his head peering over the bundles at me.

'Ah, Mr Faraday,' he barked, half-rising and holding out an emaciated hand. 'This is an unexpected pleasure.'

I was up closer now and Fogel bustled about, moving some of the papers so that he could get a clear view of me over the desk. Now that I was used to the light I could see him more clearly. I expected him to be using a quill pen but he had an ordinary ball-point in his hand as he went through some documents. He unhinged himself from his chair and came round the desk and cleared some more stuff off a high-backed chair. He looked at me cunningly over his shoulder, as he moved back to his own side.

'You haven't told my son anything of our arrangement, I hope?'

I shook my head.

'Absolute discretion, Mr Fogel. He seemed

curious, though.'

Fogel chuckled. He laid a finger alongside his nose.

'He would be.'

I sat down in the chair.

'Though I can't quite see the need for such secrecy.'

'I have my reasons,' Fogel wheezed.

He wasn't wearing his coat of assorted colours today. He had on a bottle-green creation that looked fairly modern, apart from the narrow Edwardian lapels. I didn't look too closely. The green might have been mould, after all. There was still a musty smell like cleaning fluid. He looked at me properly for the first time with his close-set grey eyes. He drew his teeth back with a sucking sound and his lean face swivelled on his neck as he took in the condition of my face.

'Good heavens, Mr Faraday,' he said. 'What have you done to yourself?'

'That's why I wanted to see you,' I said. 'Somebody didn't like me poking around Place of Hawks. He sent some muscle to bounce me around and make me lay off.'

Fogel's green face turned even greener. A strangled cackling sound came out his thin lips.

'What are you inferring, Mr Faraday?' he quavered. 'That's for you to say,' I told him.

Fogel's narrow face turned toward me as he studied me intently.

'Meaning what?'

'Meaning that there's something about Place of Hawks people don't want uncovered,' I said. 'You wouldn't know anything about that?'

Fogel shook his head.

'I don't like the implication, Mr Faraday. I was absolutely straight in what I told you. If my word will satisfy you.'

'If you say so,' I said. 'I had to be sure. There's something up there worth ten thousand dollars not to uncover.'

Fogel looked startled. His thin lips pursed in a silent whistle. He put his claw-like hands together on the blotter in front of him.

'Am I to take it that you were offered ten thousand dollars to drop the case?' he said.

I nodded. There was a strange expression in old man Fogel's eyes now.

'Whereupon you refused and were man-handled for your trouble,' he said.

'That's about it.' I said.

Fogel looked at me silently for a long moment.

'Your refusing the money and your being here leads me to assume you're still on the case?'

'You assume right,' I said. 'The roughing-up goes with the job.'

Fogel's rigid mask of a face cracked up in a brief smile. He rummaged about in the drawers of his desk.

'Ordinarily I'm not a drinking man, Mr Faraday and I don't hold with extravagance. I think on this occasion, however, we can dispense with protocol. I'd like to offer you a drink, sir.'

'And I'd be glad to accept,' I told him.

Fogel brought out a bottle and some tumblers. Glass clinked on glass.

'How much extra will the roughhouse cost me?' he said dubiously.

I almost bust out laughing. I fought to keep a straight face while the old man kept on pouring.

'The bruises are strictly on my side of the ledger,' I said.

Old man Fogey's eyes brightened. I'd swear he poured me an extra half-inch of liquor. I'd have to be watching it. Many more days on this case and I'd be turning into a lush. Fogel pushed a glass over to me.

'You'd better start at the beginning, Mr Faraday, and we'll take it from there.'

CHAPTER ELEVEN

1

I squinted through my second glass at the greenish light that spilled in at the windows.

'So you never heard of Pushkin?' I said.

Old man Fogel swivelled to and fro in his chair. He sat amid the accumulated rubbish of years as though he had all the time in the world. Twice a mousy-looking secretary had poked a startled head around the door and withdrawn baffled. I gathered that a client had never yet been seen enjoying Fogel's hospitality. I expected Fogel Jr. to come barging in any minute.

Fogel shook his head in answer to my question.

'I could find out,' he said.

'Don't bother,' I told him. 'A character like that shouldn't be too hard to trace. He's a club-owner. I'll catch up with him when I want to. Big Sam should be easier.'

Fogel watched me warily. He didn't say anything for a moment. Then he leaned forward and drained his glass. He looked regretfully at the bottle and rammed the cork home with the heel of his hand. I guessed the party was over.

'A man that size should be easier to trace than Pushkin,' he said reflectively. 'They may call on you again at your office. Have you thought of that, young man?'

'I've thought of it,' I said. 'I'll carry my gun from now on.'

Fogel looked grim. On a face like his it was really impressive.

'If things get too tough I can always find temporary space here for you,' he said.

He swept his arm round in an expansive gesture like he was offering me all the riches of Old Cathay.

'That's very nice of you,' I said.

Fogel looked at me warily. Mischief glinted somewhere in the back of his eyes.

'There'd be a small deduction from your tab,' he said. 'For the facilities provided.'

'Of course,' I said. 'I'll bear it in mind. Right now I'd like some idea of what could be so important about Place of Hawks. Is there anything on the land. Mineral rights, for instance?'

Fogel shook his head.

'Not that I ever heard of. We had the place gone over in the twenties. It beats me.'

'Well,' I said. 'We'll get to it in time. Pushkin hinted that he had a client who was interested. That could mean anything or nothing. But I can't imagine why a club-owner would be concerned.'

Fogel moistened his lips.

'You met Colonel Proctor? I hope he was helpful.'

'Very,' I said. 'He's keeping an eye open in case these people come back.'

Fogel grunted with satisfaction.

'This is all very mysterious, Mr Faraday,' he said.

'I take it you've been frank with me?' I said.

Fogel gave me a startled look. Little pink spots started out on his cheekbones.

'About Place of Hawks, Mr Faraday? Frankly, I should be annoyed at your tone, but I'm not. I find that very disturbing. I don't take to people. Usually they want something from me. Money, information or preferment in some form. You're different.'

'That's what throws you?' I said.

Fogel was silent for a long moment. He lowered his eyes down to his glass like the inch or so of liquid it contained held the information I was looking for.

'I don't know about you, Mr Faraday,' Fogel said at last. 'You're outside the usual run. And that worries me. The unknown quantity. But I know I chose the right man to crack this case. You were hinting just now that I might have been less than frank when I engaged you?'

'That's right,' I said.

Fogel chuckled. He rubbed his claw-like hands together with a low rasping like sandpaper.

'Well, Mr Faraday,' he said. 'I''ve got secrets, like most people. And lawyers have got more secrets than ordinary folk. But so far as Place of Hawks is concerned I've really no idea why people should be tramping about my property at night. Or why a man like Pushkin should have you beaten up just because you've been there.'

'Might there be anything in the property or in the history of past owners that could cause that interest?' I said.

Fogel leaned back in his chair and scratched his chin.

'The place has been in my family for a long time. I can't see where the interest would lie. But I could dig out the papers if you'd like to see them.'

I shook my head.

'Old legal documents aren't my line, Mr Fogel. But if you find anything out of the ordinary let me know.'

Fogel nodded. He cracked a thin smile suddenly.

'I could ask you to join me for lunch, Mr Faraday. But it's a bit early at eleven a.m. And I always eat sandwiches in the office.'

'Don't put yourself out,' I said. 'If you come up with anything you can always give me a ring. By the way, I met a girl near the property. She claimed to be a niece of yours.'

There was just the faintest hesitation on Fogel's part before he turned toward me. But there was no change in the intonation of his voice as he replied.

'Samantha? I haven't seen her in years. She must be a nice girl now.'

'Very nice,' I said. 'She told me her father once lived at Place of Hawks.'

'Perfectly true,' Fogel said.

He leaned back in his chair again and studied me. His face was so lean it looked paper-thin in the dim light of the office. I could see his gold watch-chain now. In the

lowered intensity of the illumination he looked younger than when I'd first seen him in my office. He was still moving his cheeks like an animal chewing grass and sucking his yellow teeth occasionally but I preferred him in low key. He looked more like an old oil painting. A Bosch of course. Not a Watteau.

He ran one of his dirty finger-nails through the patch of steel-wool on top of his skull and gave a rusty sigh.

'There was simply no reason for my not mentioning it. It didn't seem important.'

'I'll decide what's important, Mr Fogel, so long as I'm running the case,' I said.

Fogel sighed again.

'Very well, Mr Faraday,' he said in a grumbling tone. 'My brother was my partner in the firm. He lived at Place of Hawks for a while. I can't see what bearing that has . . .'

'Maybe none,' I said. 'But then again there might be some connection.'

Old man Fogel waited for me to go on.

'Suppose your brother left something in the property when he died? A will for instance. Or something valuable. The place is like a museum. And someone was trying to search the house. Or perhaps he owed money . . .'

Fogel's eyes had gone steely and glittering while I was talking. He put his hands together round the stem of his glass and looked at me bleakly.

'I didn't want to go into all this, Mr Faraday,

but since you've brought it up . . . The girl didn't say anything about her father?'

I shook my head.

'She's got tact anyway,' Fogel said.

He sucked in his cheeks again in that irritating way of his and fastened his gaze somewhere over my left shoulder. I waited for him to go on.

'There was no reason for you to know about my brother, Mr Faraday. But we've gone this far.'

The old man sighed heavily and drained the last of the liquid in his glass.

'The fact of the matter is that my brother isn't dead. Or at least we have no proof of the matter.'

I must have looked as surprised as I felt because Fogel shot me a swift glance and went on before I could interrupt.

'The truth is he simply disappeared a decade or so ago and we've never heard anything of him since. This made for a lot of difficulties in the practice, as you can imagine.'

Fogel shifted heavily in his chair.

'There was nothing wrong at all?' I said.

Fogel shook his head. His voice sounded weary as he replied.

'I thought you'd get to that. There were no missing funds and nothing irregular on Charles' side at all. After two years I had to go through legal procedures and get everything transferred to myself and my son. As the years

went by we gradually forgot Charles. Though I never ceased to wonder what had happened.'

I lit a cigarette and fished for a tray on the old man's desk. He came up with a typewriter ribbon lid that was half-full of ash and old stubs.

'What's your theory? I said.

Fogel's eyes clouded over.

'I haven't got one now,' he said. 'Though I had a dozen or so at the time. Perhaps he just got tired of the law and lit out. There was some trouble between him and his wife. They never hit it off very well.'

'What about the girl?' I said.

'He loved Samantha,' Fogel said. 'She was away at school in Europe at the time. It was two years before she came home. According to what I heard the shock stayed with her for years. I never forgave Charles for that.'

'And you never heard a word?' I said.

Fogel shook his head.

'We had the police, private enquiry agents, everybody. He just stepped out of the office one night and was never seen again. His wife never even received a postcard.'

There was a long silence between us. The atmosphere in the office seemed even more dark and forbidding than when I'd come in. I felt there was something far deeper in the set-up than old man Fogel was hinting. But it was something elusive and far-back and I didn't know in which direction to probe.

'You were fond of your brother?' I said.

Fogel's narrow head nodded assent.

'We were very close,' he said. 'And of course our working association threw us together a great deal. We had one of the biggest and best practices of its kind in the city.'

'How did you manage?' I said.

'After a few months I took my son in as a full partner,' Fogel said. 'Of course, I had to make a lot of arrangements at first. But now he's getting to be quite a useful member of the firm.'

He sniffed with a return of his old manner.

'You figure you've got enough information for one morning, Mr Faraday?'

'I never do that Mr Fogel,' I said. 'But it will do to be going on with.'

'I'd take it easy, Mr Faraday,' he said querulously. 'It appears we're stirring something up here. I don't know what but it's liable to get more dangerous than otherwise.'

'That's why I carry a Smith-Wesson,' I said. 'I'll pick it up when I get back to the office.'

'Give me a call if there's anything else I can do,' Fogel said.

'Not a word to anybody about this business,' I told him. 'Especially Colonel Proctor.'

Fogel laid his finger along his nose. A ghost of a smile came and died on his face.

'I understand,' he said.

I left him there and went on out. The throbbing in my jaws started again as I got in

the open air.

2

I sat at my old broadtop and watched sunlight quivering across cracks in the ceiling. Outside, the stalled traffic on the boulevard made a low growling noise and blinding flashes of light reflected back off the windshields. I had the windows slightly open. It was either suffocate with them closed or choke in the smog. Like always, I'd chosen the latter.

I looked at my face in the steel telephone mirror and winced. Close-up, I looked like a side of raw beef. I'd already made a few enquiries by phone but so far I hadn't been able to trace Pushkin. I'd retrieved the Smith-Wesson from the drawer of my desk and its bulk made a reassuring pressure against my chest in the nylon harness as I moved back and put my feet up. I closed my eyes and thought about the case so far and what I'd come up with. That didn't take long.

The outer door slammed and Stella came in. I'd got the worst side of my face turned away for the moment so she didn't spot the damage at first. She was wearing something that looked like a pair of flowered silk pyjamas. She had a bare midriff too, which was almost too much for me to take. The gold bell of her hair shimmered in the sunshine as she

went over to her desk and put down a leather shoulder-bag. The brown material of her trouser suit had little patterns like lizards running over it and they went into sinuous motion every time she moved.

Ordinarily I'd have admired the ingenuity but today I couldn't take it. Stella grinned like she knew what I was thinking.

'My, but we're silent today,' she said. 'Coffee?'

'Were you asking or telling?' I said.

Stella grinned again. She clopped over to the glassed-in alcove where we do the brewing-up. I heard the click as she switched the percolator on. I closed my eyes and leaned back in the chair again. Stella came back while I had my eyes closed. I heard the sharp intake of her breath as she spotted my face close-up. I opened my eyes. She bit her lip and came toward me.

'It's the way you drive, Mike,' she said mildly. 'You want to talk about it?'

'Over coffee, honey,' I said.

I put my feet down and struggled up in the chair. Stella came over and put her hand gently on the side of my face. It was cool and seemed to take all the pain away. She moved away after a minute or so and went over to the bookcase. She clicked her teeth. Cooler air started circulating as she switched on the fan.

'It's so rarely we get improvements I forgot,' I said.

116

'We'll make an exception for semi-invalids today,' Stella said.

Her blue eyes studied me anxiously as she went and sat on the edge of her desk and swung long legs.

'There was a very large gentleman here last night,' I said. 'He was about ten feet tall and five broad. He said a Mr Pushkin didn't want me nosing around Place of Hawks.'

Stella wrinkled up her forehead. It didn't spoil her looks any. She went back over to the alcove and fussed around with cups.

'So you objected and he took you apart?' she said.

'He was surprisingly gentle for his size,' I told her. 'The damage was done by a young gentleman in Pushkin's office.'

Stella reappeared at my elbow and put down a steaming cup on my blotter. I shovelled sugar in and inhaled the aroma gratefully. Stella went back to her desk and stirred her own cup.

'Hadn't you better start at the beginning?' she said.

'It's my brain,' I said. 'It's a bit addled.'

Stella made a soothing noise.

'It never was very strong,' she said.

I let that one go. I nuzzled into the java and let the warmth percolate to every corner of my body.

'The big guy blindfolded me and took me off to a club somewhere,' I said.

'You mean to say you couldn't have gotten away?' Stella said.

She sounded incredulous. 'Even if he had a gun . . .'

'He didn't need a gun,' I said. 'He almost took a policeman apart for annoying him over a fireplug. You wait until you see him.'

'I hope I don't,' Stella said, 'if that's what he's like.'

'He might call around again,' I said.

I downed a few more mouthfuls of coffee, added a mite more sugar to my cup. Stella sat and watched me with that consummate tact of hers.

'Anyway, we got to this club and I met Moses Pushkin,' I said. 'He offered me ten thousand fish to lay off the case.'

'We could have done with the money, Mike,' Stella reminded me.

'Not that sort of money,' I said. 'Besides, I really want to know what's going on up at Place of Hawks.'

'I'd like to know too,' Stella said. 'I haven't seen you for thirty-six hours.'

'All in good time,' I said. 'Pushkin got annoyed when I wouldn't play ball and had one of his boys rough me up. Then Kong brought me back to my car.'

Stella tossed her head impatiently and picked up her cup again.

'What did you find out about Mr Fogel's estate, Mike?' she said.

'I'll give you the set-up in a minute,' I said. 'Just as soon as I've finished my second cup of coffee.'

CHAPTER TWELVE

1

Stella cupped her chin on her hands and looked at me seriously. It was almost dusk now and green, blue and red neon were burning holes in the shadows of the boulevard below the window. She'd filled half a dozen pages of her notebook and the air was thick with my cigarette smoke. It was long past Stella's quitting time. I like to run a neat set-up and I didn't want to take advantage of her good nature. Not businesswise, anyway. I looked at her bare midriff again and jerked my mind back to business.

The fan was chopping the ragged edges of the smoke clouds to tatters but the air was getting pretty close for all that. I went over to open the window facing the boulevard to let a little of the smoke escape.

'What are you doing for food, Mike?' Stella said.

'I'll grab a sandwich somewhere,' I said. 'I'd take you out to dinner but I'm not sure it's safe.'

Stella closed up her notebook and tidied her desk. I stood at the window watching the boulevard. I heard her put the hood over her typewriter.

'That's what worries me, Mike,' she said. 'Do you think Pushkin knows you've been to see Fogel?'

'He might,' I said. 'He had me tailed before.'

I turned to face Stella across the room. Only the desk lamp was on and the upper part of her body was in shadow so I couldn't read her expression.

'This is a tough one,' I said. 'My guess is the answer's somewhere in L.A. And it takes too much time to keep flogging up to Place of Hawks.'

'Couldn't you stay at Colonel Proctor's?' Stella said.

She sat down again as I went over to my desk.

'I might take up his hospitality for a day or two,' I said. 'But it's a funny set-up there.'

Stella grinned suddenly.

'At least his sister and the girl would be safe from you,' she said.

'That's what bothers me,' I said. 'They're both pretty attractive.'

Stella let that one go.

'You want me to take a look around when I leave?' she said.

'It might be helpful,' I told her.

120

Stella picked up her shoulder-bag. She switched off the desk lamp. There was just the light from the waiting room now, making a yellow slice of illumination across the office, mingling with the coloured segments from the neon signs. She came across and put her face up against mine. I stood it for a moment or two but she skipped away too quickly for me.

'Take care, Mike,' she said. 'I'll ring in about ten minutes.'

I sat and watched her walk away through the waiting room. I heard the door latch behind her and then her footsteps died away down the corridor. Presently I heard the whine of the elevator going down. I was left alone with the faint frittering of the fan, the night and the neons. I got back up and watched the boulevard from the window. I saw a faint figure which could have been Stella walk down the block.

At almost the same time someone got out a parked automobile which was in front of a drugstore almost opposite our building. It may have been coincidence. Or not. I watched until both figures had disappeared around the corner. Then I closed and locked the window and switched the fan off. I kept on watching. The figure came back to the automobile and climbed in. He was holding something which looked like a newspaper. The car remained in front of the building. The phone buzzed just then.

'A dark-haired man followed me just now,' Stella said. 'He got out a gold-coloured Packard just across from our entrance. He followed me for a block and then went back. I think he might be your man.'

'Nice going, honey,' I said. 'I think you're right. And thanks.'

'Watch out, Mike,' Stella said. She put the phone down.

2

I went back over to the window. The Packard was still there. I could see the faint glow of the driver's cigarette. I checked on the Smith-Wesson, put it in my right-hand trouser pocket and kept my hand on the butt. I switched off the rest of the lights and locked the office. The elevator wasn't working now so I walked down to the ground floor.

I waited until a group of people passed the entrance and then drifted out. I paused and looked in the lit window of a travel agency. I could see the other side of the boulevard reflected clearly. The driver of the Packard had got out and was waiting for a break in the traffic to cross. He'd taken the bait. I grinned and walked on slowly, giving him time to catch up.

I walked toward my usual garage as though I were going to pick up the Buick. I turned the

corner of a building and in at the loading bay of a small warehouse. There were several frame buildings in here, set at right-angles and plenty of room to manoeuvre. I picked my way through piles of crates. The engine of a truck throbbed in the evening air and the yellow light from warehouse interiors sliced across the gloom.

I got round behind an aisle of crates and watched the sidewalk. I was about twenty feet away and well in the shadow. The figure of a tall, strongly-built man in a light blue suit passed across my field of vision. He had dark glossy hair and something about the way he held himself reminded me of the big guy in Pushkin's office.

I couldn't be sure. It was just a hunch. I waited for five minutes. Muffled conversation and the beat of hurrying footsteps came from the sidewalk. Then I saw the big man again. He slipped round the edge of the warehouse wall, and eased into the yard so silently and quickly that I almost took his figure for the shadow of a man passing on the boulevard outside. He was a professional all right. He'd gone on, found he'd lost me and come back to the only place I could have turned off. It was what I would have done myself.

I studied the terrain. All the time he stayed on the other side of the yard I was safe. There was a broad band of light from the warehouse doors farther down which stretched almost to

where I was standing. I'd no doubt in my own mind what the set-up was. I'd been given a warning last night. I'd ignored the warning and gone to see Fogel. If these characters were keeping close tabs on me and all the evidence pointed to that, they'd know. There wouldn't be any more interviews or offers.

The big man in the Packard meant business. I could easily avoid him now by ducking out but it wouldn't solve anything. They'd still be after me. And Big Sam would still be around. A man like Pushkin could hire a dozen tough bimbos to deal with a character like me. Anyways, I was tired of being pushed around. It was time to hit back and prove I meant business too. Besides, I wanted to question the black-haired character. He'd give me a direct lead to Pushkin if I could make him talk.

I got down behind the crates as a diesel gunned out. The headlights swept across the sheeted bodies of a couple of trucks parked opposite. I spotted the legs of the dark man then, halfway along the bulk of the second truck. He was working his way farther up the yard. I got the Smith-Wesson out and went back along the aisle of crates, keeping level with him. I heard the sound of voices then and there came the faint, unmistakeable smell of cigar smoke. Cheap cigar smoke at that.

Two men in dark coveralls were coming across the yard from the direction of the warehouses. They were arguing about baseball

scores and I could hear their strong Irish-American accents clearly in the warm air. I couldn't see the big man now. He'd probably gone to ground behind the trucks. There was another tangle of crates behind me and I got back into them and away from the aisle where people were more likely to pass to and fro.

I waited a few more seconds. The two men passed me and went off toward the entrance of the yard and disappeared along the sidewalk. There was still light coming from the warehouse doors farther down. I picked up the big man again then. He'd gone to ground behind the second truck and was evidently getting his bearings. Something was puzzling him. I could almost read his mind. He was working out whether I'd gone straight through the yard and out the other side.

Supposing I could have found an exit. Or whether I was hanging around to get the drop on him. It was the old feeling of the hunter. I decided to give him some help. I picked up a pebble from among the crates at my feet and lobbed it along the yard. It hit the ground about thirty feet from where I was standing. The big man whirled behind the truck body. I could almost see his feet leave the ground. He started to go around the truck bonnet fast.

I crossed the yard while he was doing that and got in behind the tailboard of the second truck. I eased around the end and looked along to where the big man had been standing.

The light was dimmer here but there was just enough for me to see that he was no longer there. I was now behind him and the advantage was with me. I held the Smith-Wesson in my right hand and went forward, taking care not to scrape it against the woodwork of the truck.

There was no sign of the big man now. Presumably he was across the other side of the yard, somewhere up near the warehouse doors. Unaware that I was behind him. Leastways, I hoped so. I crept on down toward the second truck. There was a patch of shadow halfway and I wondered for a minute whether the big man had doubled back between the two trucks. That was something I should have to watch.

I waited a few seconds longer and then crept forward again. I was within the patch of shadow and I could see that the man with the glossy hair was nowhere around. I dropped to the ground and wormed my way along. There was no sign of his feet the other side of the truck. I nearly made a fatal mistake then. I straightened up and worked nearer to the front of the truck. I heard the faint click of a door handle. I dropped back to the ground.

The big man had a feeling something wasn't quite right. Instead of following up the sound of the pebble hitting the ground he'd done the opposite thing. He'd gone around the end of the truck bonnet all right. But instead of

crossing the yard he'd stood on the running board of the vehicle where I couldn't see his feet if I looked underneath. Now he was easing into the offside door of the cab. He expected me to pass by and then he'd blast me from behind.

I grinned in the semi-darkness. The grin was probably a trifle crooked. I'd almost underestimated him. I'd wondered why he hadn't brought Big Sam along. The answer was that a pro. like him didn't need Big Sam. I eased back along the edge of the truck and waited. Distant voices still came from the open doors of the warehouses and I could see shadows silhouetted against the light of the loading bays. There was a long pause. I threw off the safety of the Smith-Wesson. A fly buzzed suddenly in the silence and I could feel sweat trickling down my back.

There came again the same clicking noise. I watched the cab door. A dark shadow grew with infinite slowness. The door was opening fraction by fraction as the man crouched inside the cab put stealthy pressure on it. I could see the faint outline of a thumb against the edge of the metal now. That would be to prevent any noise if the door slipped back. I had an idea then. I eased forward. The opening door suddenly stopped. Perhaps my shoe had made the faintest scraping noise along the ground. I stayed where I was.

The cab door hovered and then slowly

127

closed. I'd missed my opportunity to crush the big man's thumb. I ducked down and went around the front of the cab, crouching low under the bonnet, where I wouldn't be seen. I looked around. My shadow was beneath the body of the truck. I eased around the radiator grille just in time to see the offside door swinging open. The big man was uncannily silent in his movements but the advantage was with me.

3

I went at the cab with a rush, my shoulder swinging the heavy metal door inwards on its hinges. I heard the big man grunt with pain as he went over backwards. I had the door open now and levered up into the interior; I flailed with the Smith-Wesson at the shadowy figure inside, felt the barrel connect with flesh and bone. The man with the glossy hair went over again; I heard a heavy thud as his gun fell on to the wooden floor of the cab. He got his foot into my chest before I could get across the seat cushions.

I saw the light from the warehouse doors describe a crazy arc as I went through the air. I landed heavily on my shoulders, rolled over in the dust. I kept hold of the Smith-Wesson. I heard the engine of the truck growl into life then. Yellow light stabbed across the yard.

There were faint shouts from the direction of the warehouse. The light blinded me as I tried to crawl away. I was winded and couldn't make good time.

I heard the engine of the truck accelerate and then the heavy vibration as it shook the ground. The big man was sending it straight for me. I got off one shot in the direction of the headlamps, heard glass crack somewhere. One of the lights blinked out. I rolled again, got in behind some crates as the big truck slewed crazily and skidded broadside as the driver tried to follow me. There was a rending crack as the bodywork tore at the angled steel girder frames at the corner of the building.

I could see the shadows of the men in the warehouse. They were running back inside the doorway. I was up now. The truck engine gunned again as the big man reversed the heavy diesel. There came the screaming of metal as he dragged it back away from the tangle of crates and girders. I could see the faint shadow behind the windshield. I jumped back into the darkness where the warehouse wall came down to the ground and snapped off another shot. The windscreen starred and there came an answering spat of flame from the cab.

I felt the hot breath of the bullet and something sparked off the metal sheeting near my shoulder. I changed position again as the truck thundered up toward me. I could hear a

faint sound like a patrol wagon siren now, coming from across town. The man in the truck must have heard it too. The big machine lumbered up toward me, its single yellow headlight looking like a malevolent eye in the gloom of the yard.

There was another shot and I saw the cab door swing wide. Glossy hair was trying to pin me with the truck. Failing that he'd jump off and get me as I ducked for cover. I didn't wait. I put two shots of my remaining three through the door panel. I heard the slam of the bullets almost before the reports stung my eardrums. A darker shadow detached itself from the truck cab and rolled over in the dust toward me.

I got the hell out as the big machine careered into a pile of crates to my right front. I tripped and fell as the mountain of cases started erupting. The drumming of the truck tyres went on and the engine was screaming on a high note. I got up and went over toward the black shape sprawled in the dirt. The big man looked like he was crucified onto the ground.

The yellow pencil of the truck headlight, tilted skyward now, made a yellow mask of his face. Black shadow crawled from the corner of his mouth and made a pool at his side. The big cannon he'd been using lay three yards from him. I kicked it away but he was in no state to use it. The voices were louder now. I wouldn't have long. The man with glossy hair opened

his eyes. I couldn't read their expression. He choked for a moment. I leaned down until I could whisper in his ear.

'Where can I find Pushkin? I said.

The big man shook his head slowly. Perspiration cascaded down his cheeks. He made strangling noises low down in his throat.

'Astor . . .' he started to say.

He changed his mind, tried to spit in my face. Then he died.

I got up and dusted myself down. The noise of the siren was a lot louder. I could hear running feet over the throbbing of the diesel motor. I got down the aisle behind the crates. I put the Smith-Wesson away as I ran. I found a small door that led out the yard and went two blocks before I let up. I dusted myself down, using my reflection in a shop window. When I felt I was respectable I got in a booth in a drug-store and rang Stella and told her what had happened.

It was now almost eight o'clock. I called Samantha Fogel. I had to wait almost five minutes before she answered. It seemed a long time. I couldn't go to my Park West house, the office or Stella's. Either Pushkin's boys or the police would want to see me. Probably both.

'I've got a big favour to ask you, Miss Fogel,' I said, after I'd identified myself. The girl must have been clairvoyant. Her voice was like music in my ears.

'You'd like to come on up?' she said.

'Tonight,' I said. 'It's pretty urgent or I wouldn't have bothered you.'

'That's all right, Mr Faraday,' the girl said. 'If it's anything to do with Place of Hawks it's important to me.'

'Fine,' I said. 'This time of night I could be there by half-eleven if you tell me how to find the house.'

'I'll be waiting,' Samantha Fogel said. 'Just start driving.'

CHAPTER THIRTEEN

1

It was just a quarter to twelve when the Buick's wheels rumbled over the approach drive to the girl's place. Following her instructions I'd found a side road leading off to the left about a mile before the Place of Hawks. It was a lonely spot and the Buick rocked round the curves, the beat of the motor echoing back from limestone cliffs and reverberating across the countryside. Cicadas were chirping loudly and somewhere far-off I could hear running water.

I had the window down and the air, cooler now, and bringing with it the scent of grass and flowers, felt good against my battered face. I glanced at myself in the mirror, switching on

132

the interior light momentarily, and saw that most of the swelling had gone down.

The Fogel girl's place was a big, ranch-style spread, surrounded with a white picket fence. My headlights picked out the long, low white building and about an acre of lawn that stretched down toward the entrance gate. There were lights on in the lower storey of the house and as the tyres crunched over the gravelled drive a brass lantern winked into life on the porch.

Samantha Fogel waved and came down the broad entrance steps as I killed the motor and the silence crowded back in. I got out the car and slammed the door. It sounded like an intrusion in that atmosphere. Then the noise of frogs and night creatures started up again. The girl came forward and gave me a small brown hand to shake.

'I'm glad you could come, Mr Faraday,' she said. 'I've wanted to talk to you ever since we met.'

'Even at this time of night?' I said. 'I'm afraid I haven't brought any things.'

'Oh, I expect we can fix you up,' the girl said easily. 'Mother's gone to bed but your room's ready. Have you eaten?'

I shook my head. We were up on the stoop by this time and the girl gave a little sharp exclamation as she took in the state of my face.

'Tell you about it later,' I said. 'If you've got anything ready I'd be grateful. I'm starving.'

The girl smiled.

'Just what I figured,' she said.

We were in a pitch-pine hall with polished Colonial furniture now. She locked and bolted the heavy oak door behind us. A big sheepdog with cadging brown eyes made its lazy way toward us as the girl ushered me through another door. I took in more old furniture, polished oak floors and something I hadn't seen in years; one of those nineteenth-century spinning wheels. I went over and sat in a rocker with burnished mahogany staves set beside a large brick fireplace while the girl went through the far door. I heard a light-switch click and then the girl was calling from the kitchen.

'Drinks on the sideboard if you want. I'll join you in something long and cool. You'll find all the things there. Mother said she'll be glad to meet you at breakfast.'

'She hasn't seen me yet,' I said.

The girl laughed. I wandered over to the sideboard and switched on a shaded lamp that stood at one end of it. I poured myself a scotch and stirred some ice into it with a glass mixing rod. I felt my jangled nerves settling at the first sip. The girl was behind me now, laying the round oak dining table for two. She touched a bottle with one hand as she passed by.

'And not too much ice,' she called. 'If you want to wash up Prince will show you the way. It's out in the hall.'

I poured the Fogel girl's drink and followed the ambling bulk of the sheepdog. He stopped before a door near the staircase and looked back over his shoulder at me pityingly. I thanked him and went on in. I had a look at myself in the mirror over the washbasin. I didn't spend too long over it. Then I ran a cold tap over my head and scrubbed my hands. I found a stiff brush hanging over to one side and removed the dust of travel. After that I felt considerably improved. I only looked like the victim of an auto wreck now. While I was in the wash-room I broke out some spare slugs from my shoulder holster and re-loaded the Smith-Wesson. I'd be going up to Place of Hawks again in the morning.

The dog was waiting at the door when I got there and led the way back to the dining room. The Fogel girl had set out blue flowered plates which shone under the central brass lamp hanging from the ceiling beams and there was everything a hungry private dick could have wished for. Including a number of intangible expressions in the girl's eyes. She shovelled ham and eggs onto my plate and leaned over to pour the steaming black coffee from an earthenware pot.

She looked slightly different from the last time I'd seen her though she was still informally dressed. She wore a faded blue shirt and tailored jeans and her feet were bare above the red leather slippers. She still wore

the gold chain with the medallion and it strained forward over her taut breasts as she finished pouring the coffee. She turned over a cup that had been inverted on its saucer and poured herself one. I guessed that the table had been laid for breakfast. I caught a glimpse of a comfortable, ordered life. The kind I'd likely never be having.

Her smooth brown hair, sleek with health, was still tied in the pony-tail and her cornflower-blue eyes looked at me candidly as I fooled with my bread-roll and prepared to dive into the ham and eggs. Her face looked browner than ever under the soft sheen of the overhead lamp.

'I'd say you were a man in some trouble, Mr Faraday,' she said.

'You'd probably be right, Miss Fogel,' I said. 'Right now I'm wondering just why you weren't more surprised when I phoned so late.'

The girl smiled again, more faintly this time.

'I've learned not to be surprised at many things in the past ten years,' she said. 'I just had a hunch. It's about Place of Hawks, isn't it?'

'Looks that way,' I said, spearing a mouthful of ham. It was great.

The girl sat back and cradled her slim fingers round her earthenware coffee-cup.

'Perhaps we'd better wait until you've eaten,' she said. 'In the meantime I'll go put your car away.'

'The key's in the ignition,' I said.

I watched her cross the room with lithe, easy movements. She made hardly a sound over the uncarpeted oak floor. The big dog sniffed at me superciliously and then followed the girl out. I went on shovelling ham and eggs down my throat.

2

I heard the Buick growl away around the corner of the house. I'd finished the eggs and was on my second cup of coffee by the time she came back. She went out and returned with a slice of home-made apple pie and cream. She put it down in front of me and cut herself a slice.

'Cheese on the dish if you want anything more,' the girl said.

I began to feel like a character out of Rebecca of Sunnybrook Farm.

'This is just fine,' I told her.

She was silent until I'd finished. Then we took the coffee cups and jug over to the seats by the fireplace. There wasn't any fire of course, but it seemed the natural thing to do. The girl took a gold-plated lighter off an occasional table and lit my cigarette for me. Up close she looked even more sensational than from a distance. I offered her my pack. She shook her head, flicked the lighter shut

and sat down again.

'Shall I start or will you?' she said.

'It's my case. I'll make the running,' I said. 'Someone tried to kill me tonight. It's connected with Place of Hawks. I'd like somewhere to hide out for a few days.'

'You've got it,' the girl said calmly, as if she had visitors like me every afternoon. She folded one elegant leg over the other and searched my face with her eyes.

'I don't think you quite understand, Miss Fogel,' I said.

The girl interrupted me. 'Samantha. And I think I understand perfectly. You don't want to go into details?'

I shook my head. I leaned back in my chair and feathered smoke at the ceiling beams.

'Not for the moment,' I said.

The girl shrugged slightly.

'Ethics or something else?' she said.

'A little of both,' I told her. 'Let's level, shall we. My guess is you've got a key to Place of Hawks? Right? If you weren't up there someone was because I heard them on several occasions.'

There was a long silence. The girl had turned very pink. Her complexion was back to normal before she replied.

'I do have a key, Mr Faraday. There was no reason really for me to lie, except that I didn't know you very well.'

'You don't know me any better now,' I said.

'Our acquaintance is only an hour older.'

The girl shook her head.

'I'm a pretty good judge of character and I've been thinking things over since we first met. But before I open out I have to remember you're representing Uncle Adelbert.'

'And you don't like him very much?' I finished for her. 'You needn't worry about that. I never let clients get in the way of the truth.'

The girl expelled her breath in a little sigh.

'I was hoping you'd say that. I used to live at Place of Hawks, as I told you. I loved the property when we all lived there. After Daddy disappeared—when I got back from Europe, I found a key. The place had been let to an aunt by then. Naturally, I could go up there any time. Then she died and the place was locked up and allowed to decay. I remembered the key.'

'So you go up there and cook meals?' I said.

The girl looked at me shrewdly.

'You still don't quite understand, Mr Faraday. Someone else goes up there and watches an empty house and grounds. And cooks for himself with the stuff in the kitchen.'

There was another long silence.

'What's your theory?' I said.

Samantha Fogel drew her chair nearer to me.

'Maybe when I find what I'm looking for I'll

have the answer to that, too.'

'Just what are you looking for?' I said.

'Evidence, facts about my father's death,' the girl said. 'Somewhere in that house I'm convinced is a clue to the way Daddy disappeared. He must be dead, of course; he would have contacted us years ago if it were humanly possible.'

'And you suspect old man Fogel of having something to do with it?'

Samantha looked moodily at the toe of one of her red slippers.

'It would have been to his advantage,' she said. 'The practice was an enormously rich one. And there would have been more for him and his son.'

I got up and tapped off the ash in a crystal tray on the far side of the low table.

'It seems pretty far-fetched, Miss Fogel,' I said.

'Samantha,' the girl corrected me.

'Samantha,' I said. 'Why would one brother kill another? Even for money it doesn't add up.'

'How long have you been a private eye?' the girl said.

I sat down again.

'All right,' I said. 'Maybe it does make sense. And maybe I just don't want to think about that angle. Why would old man Fogel want himself investigated?'

'Because the Colonel had seen me snooping

around up here,' the girl said calmly. 'That's leaving aside the presence of a third person. Doesn't it seem strange to you that my uncle never sold the property? Even as it stands Place of Hawks must be worth a fortune. Could it be he let it become derelict because he daren't let a stranger live there? And that he's searching for something in the house belonging to Daddy?'

She'd got a good point there. I didn't answer right away but just let my cigarette burn down before stubbing it out in the tray.

'You've been seeing too many re-runs of Gaslight on television,' I said.

The girl smiled a far-away smile like the matter was too serious for joking. That wasn't very hard to believe either.

'There's another point,' I said. 'If the Colonel saw you why didn't he simply tell the old man it was a girl? He would soon have connected you with the house.'

Samantha Fogel shook her head.

'I never let anyone get close. I know the estate too well. The Colonel might have seen my car going down the back road. But most likely he simply saw lights. And that would be very rare because I usually do my snooping in daytime.'

'We'll let that go,' I said. 'Next question. Why would Fogel let Place of Hawks to a relative if he was afraid of something being discovered up there?'

The girl tapped with slim fingers on the rim of her coffee-cup.

'That's the trump card, Mr Faraday,' she said. 'The perfect cover. The only sort of person Uncle Adelbert could have let the house to. Aunt Muriel was blind.'

There was another long silence.

'You've got an answer for everything,' I said.

The girl smiled, showing perfect teeth.

'Convinced?'

'Not yet,' I said. 'But you're making a good case.'

Samantha Fogel frowned at the ceiling. She was behaving as though we were old friends. The funny thing was I had the same impression. Though I was working for old man Fogel all her assumptions seemed to have good points behind them. But I wasn't entirely sold.

'Aunt Muriel had only an elderly companion living in the house,' the girl said. 'Other help came in on a daily or weekly basis from the village.'

I looked inquiringly at her.

'There's a small settlement about a mile farther down from here,' she said.

'You're sure you're levelling with me?' I said. 'This isn't just a test for old man Fogel?'

The girl looked at me sharply. She wriggled her toes in the red slippers.

'I could be offended at that,' she said calmly. 'But I won't be. I told you I loathe the

142

old man. If you won't help me find out what's going on up at the house then I'll carry on on my own.'

'I didn't say I wouldn't help you,' I said. 'Though I can't work for two people at once. But there's nothing to stop you stringing along. Whatever we find out we split fifty-fifty.'

I got up and walked over to the window. The lights still burned on the porch. Otherwise, there was nothing but the night and far away a few pinpricks of light. That would be the village the girl had spoken about.

Samantha Fogel got up and came over to my side. The top of her head came almost up to my chin. That's the way I like them. Her hair smelled of perfume and warm grass. I was having difficulty in concentrating on the case with her so close.

'It's a deal, Michael,' she said.

'Mike,' I told her.

'Mike,' she repeated.

She looked at my face quizzically.

'You still wouldn't care to tell me how you got that hammering?'

'I'll save it for later,' I said. 'It will give us something to do when the evenings get cooler.'

I sighed.

'We shall probably have plenty of time. If you've been up there for months and found nothing what am I likely to turn up?'

The girl put a hand out and ran it lightly over my face, like she was trying to smooth its

143

battered contours.

'We'll just have to wait and see,' she said.

CHAPTER FOURTEEN

1

The sun shimmered back blindly off the windows of Place of Hawks as the girl and I eased our way up through the undergrowth of the back road. We'd left her car half a mile off and walked in in order not to advertise our presence. It was only nine a.m. but already heat was rising in visible waves from the ground and blurring the far distance.

This morning some of Samantha Fogel's suppositions didn't seem quite so offbeat as the previous night. In fact she'd given me a few ideas. Some of the answers to my problems were undoubtedly in L.A. But an equal number could be here. I wished I knew what we were looking for.

The key to Pushkin's interest in the property could lie in a document; an object; or an idea. And the house was a vast place where one could wander for days without coming up with the right slant.

I looked at the girl as we ducked under the fallen tree and came up closer to the rear of the mansion. None of my doubts showed on

her face at any rate. This morning she still wore the jeans but this time with a tan-coloured silk shirt that was every bit as sensational as her other outfits.

We'd had breakfast with her mother at seven a.m.; Mrs Fogel was a quiet woman with a face which still bore the remains of a striking beauty; though she was kind and animated enough to my eyes she seemed to carry the burden of her secret sorrow as an ever present presence. I guessed then that the girl's life hadn't been an easy one. I understood something of her obsession with the missing father. Both she and her mother were resigned to the thought of his death but the secret behind his disappearance was something that gnawed at them constantly.

The girl glanced at me like she could read my thoughts. We were close up to the big porch entrance by this time. By coming over the waist-high grass and crouching low we couldn't be seen from the driveway.

'I don't quite know why we're doing this,' the girl said.

I shrugged.

'Just a hunch. We don't want to advertise our presence. I thought you wanted to be inconspicuous.'

Samantha Fogel made a little face.

'I usually reconnoitre the road first and then go in back. There's an unlocked window there.'

'I thought you had a front door key,' I said.

'That's for after dark,' the girl said.

'We'll use the front today,' I said. 'We haven't got time to fool around. Whoever's in back of all this is afraid of my finding out something. He won't waste any time either, not now he knows I'm still alive.'

The girl smiled faintly. I noticed her breathing was a little deeper than usual. Her breasts rose and fell gently beneath the silk shirt.

'Good reasoning, Mike.'

'It's my business,' I said modestly. 'Whoever comes up here has to have a car. It's my bet he comes out from L.A. In which case it's a little early in the morning for his arrival. And if we're inside and anyone shows up we shall hear.'

The girl followed me as I crossed the drive and got in under the porch. There was no sign of any recent car-tracks in the gravel. The sun was hot on my shoulder blades as I waited for a moment or two. The trees in the distance shimmered in the heat and the drive curved off until it was lost in the cool dimness of the foliage. I got out my key and opened the big door. Once again we were back in the Citizen Kane entrance hall. I closed the door quietly behind us. The sound seemed to make a dull whisper in the far corners of the house.

'You know the place better than I do,' I said. 'It's your show.'

The girl tossed her head.

'I've been over most of the lay-out,' she said. 'There's the cellars and the stable-wing.'

'Sounds promising,' I said.

We were interrupted by the ringing of a bell from somewhere in the house. It came from the ground floor and it sounded like an exaggerated version of a telephone. There was a strange expression in the girl's eyes as she came up close to me.

'Are my ears going or is that a phone?' I said.

Samantha Fogel had a look of muted triumph on her face.

'Your ears are all right, Mike,' she said. 'It's just what I've been asking myself. Why a working telephone in an empty house? And why one with a specially loud tone? To call somebody from far off perhaps?'

'Have you ever tried to answer it?' I said.

The girl shook her head.

'Every time it rang off before I got there.'

'I heard it when I was here last time,' I said. 'Let's see what happens.'

The girl turned and went away across the hall.

'It's in the big salon over here,' she said. 'There's another upstairs but it only rings down here.'

The ringing sounded again. It seemed like a firebell in the hushed silence of the house. The phone was a big Edwardian thing with

147

chromed earpieces and a fluted rest on a heavy stand. It clicked as I picked it up and the bell cut off. I put my handkerchief over the mouthpiece and motioned the girl to silence. There was a sort of Edwardian silence in the earpiece too.

I made a non-committal noise into the handkerchief. There was a dry cough from the other end of the phone.

'Ah, I'm glad I caught you in time.'

It was a young man's voice, anxious and tense.

'I had things to do,' I said.

There was a sudden pause and I could sense the suspicion flowing in at the other end.

'Are you still there?' I said.

There was a metallic click and the line was full of crackling emptiness. I sighed and put the receiver back on the cradle.

'Interesting but inconclusive,' I said. 'But it gives me ideas. Someone's expected up here. They evidently haven't arrived. Which gives us time to prepare.'

The girl looked agitated.

'We can't hang around here, Mike,' she said, indicating the big, empty room with its chairs shrouded in dust sheets.

'Shall we try the cellars?'

'Sounds great,' I said. 'But what about our friend?'

Samantha Fogel shrugged.

'We don't know for sure if anyone's turning

148

up. And we're bound to hear a car.'

'What can we lose?' I said.

2

I followed the girl out into the hall and down the familiar corridor which led to the gymnasium where I'd first met the Colonel. Although I'd only been up here once before I was beginning to feel like I'd known the place for years. Our footsteps echoed under the high ceiling as we passed the doors I'd already looked through.

'There's a big central heating plant down below,' the girl said. 'I first went down the cellar to check if it was still working. Whoever uses the kitchen would find it pretty cold up here in the mountains during the winter without the heating.'

'And was it?' I said.

The girl nodded.

'Not only was everything in first class order but the oil-tank was full.'

'It might have been left over from when your aunt died,' I said.

Samantha Fogel frowned to herself.

'She died at the end of the winter,' she said. 'The tank was nearly empty. I know because I used to check on it for her. Can you imagine my uncle spending money to heat an empty house?'

I scratched my chin with the edge of my thumb.

'It doesn't add up,' I said. 'Why are we going to the cellars now?'

'Because they're full of junk,' the girl said. 'Crates, furniture, old desks, bundles of documents. I haven't had time to go through any of it yet.'

She led the way across the gymnasium to a small oak door set in the far wall. Our feet stirred up dust as well as echoes from the high ceiling. I remembered the afternoon I'd met the Colonel here. It was only a short while ago but it seemed like weeks. Place of Hawks had that effect on one. Time seemed to stand still up here and an afternoon dragged out like a month in any other place. Samantha Fogel thumbed an old-fashioned brass switch screwed to the wall and led the way down. I'd already put the lights on at the main when we came in.

The stair treads were made of oak and beautifully dovetailed; the sort of craftsman-ship you don't see nowadays. It was all of a piece with the rest of the house; everything had to be just right, even in the cellars. The stairs wound down and we came to a large open space. Two bare light bulbs burned dustily, hanging from the beams of the floor above. They cast a shadowed brilliance over heaps of coke in a bunker at one side. A large oil-burning furnace stood over against one

wall. There was nothing else in the room except for a couple of old cane chairs, one reversed on the other, which stood over near the coal-bunker.

Samantha Fogel led the way over to a door of rough planking just beyond the furnace. She opened it and fumbled with another switch. A second flight of wooden steps led down until they disappeared beneath another door which shone dully in the harsh light of the overhead bulbs. There was something curious about the door but I couldn't make it out until I got up to it. The girl had stopped and was searching for a key in the pocket of her jeans. The walls were stone here and cold seemed to flow out of them.

I touched the door curiously with a finger-tip as the girl struggled to turn the big key in the lock. It appeared to be made of solid metal. The sill and surrounds were of the same metal and rebated into the walls themselves. As the girl opened the door I saw it was about four inches thick. The walls themselves were granite and about three feet thick. Samantha Fogel looked at me curiously as I paused in the doorway.

'There's something screwy here,' I said. 'Why the Fort Knox set-up for a coal cellar?'

The girl had gone down a few steps in front of me but now she came back. She frowned interrogatively. I pushed the door with the flat of my palm. It went round on well-oiled

hinges. I could see now it was made of solid steel.

'This was built in my aunt's time,' she said. 'On Mr Fogel's orders, I believe. My uncle used to store a lot of the more valuable furniture and pictures down here.'

I stood looking at the dull sheen of the massive door. The air from the vault seemed to press in on us now with cool, probing fingers.

'There's something doesn't sit right, honey,' I said. 'No one would go to all this trouble just to store stuff in a cellar. How come you got a key?'

'I found this in an old box after my aunt's death,' Samantha Fogel said. 'It was in a small wall-safe in her bedroom. I guess it must have been overlooked.'

She looked at me with those cornflower-blue eyes I was beginning to find a little unnerving. The light from the naked bulbs shimmered back from the rich mass of her dark brown hair as she shifted her position on the steps. She gave the big door a worried look.

'I never thought about it before. Now you mention it, I suppose it might seem strange. Unless there's something else down here.'

'That's what we came to find out, wasn't it?' I said.

Samantha Fogel turned and went down the remaining stairs with easy, graceful

movements as I followed her. The cellar here was a huge, pillared place, full of shadows and dim corners. It was also full of furniture which sat like deserted ghosts under white sheeting; I could see the light reflecting back off the gilt of picture-frames and the heavy moulding of candelabra. It looked like a scene from a Buñuel film. I whistled softly in the cool dimness.

'It will take months to sift this stuff through,' I said.

The girl's gold medallion swung impatiently against her neck as she turned back to me.

'We've got to start somewhere, Mike.'

She had a point. I left her standing by a tall mirror in a bevelled frame which was so thick with dust it couldn't throw back a reflection any more. The cellar was only partly underground at this point. There was a small window up near the ceiling, about a foot square, which had been boarded over. A single ray of sunshine escaped and scratched a golden beam across the interior of the cellar.

Workmen had been constructing something here; there was a framework of heavy timber at the side of the wall, a jumble of tools and wood-shavings littering the floor. I scraped my size nines on the ground and watched a slow spiral of dust ascend into the single beam of light. I worked my way round the cellar and back up toward the girl. She stood where she was, her face in shadow under the overhead

bulb, and stared at the dusty mirror as though it could tell us something. I could have done with some answers myself because nothing which had happened on this case so far made any sense at all.

We were still standing like that when there came a crash which echoed through the cellar. I was already up the first flight of wooden steps before the sound had stopped vibrating in our eardrums. I heard a key turn in the lock before I got to the big steel door. I knew it was hopeless even before I put my shoulder to it.

CHAPTER FIFTEEN

1

Samantha Fogel's face was ashen as she joined me in front of the great burnished slab of metal. She looked at the door sombrely as though she could will herself through it. I felt her body tremble as she put her arm on mine.

'Would it help any, Mike, if I said I was sorry?' she said in a low voice.

'It might but I doubt it,' I said. 'Save it for when we're out of here.'

I had my ear to the panel and heard the faint, far-off slam of the door to the outer cellar. I had the Smith-Wesson out now and I ran down the steps again, leaving the girl

twisting uselessly at the handle. I jumped up on to the baulks of timber the workmen had left. There were a lot of crates and other stuff here and I moved cautiously up toward the rear wall where the single ray of light shone.

I found I was sweating as I got up close to it. The window was close-boarded and the big nails had been hammered home into the heavy wood surround. I went back down below and rummaged around in the tools. I found a pick and took that back up to the window. The girl stood and watched me like she was carved in stone. I didn't say anything. I levered with the broad, flat edge of the pick against the boarding.

It creaked and then the nails gave with a scream. Light streamed into the cellar as I levered the covering back and let it fall to the ground. I heard the girl gasp as I uncovered the opening. The window was no more than a foot square. It went through two feet thick stone and ended up in a heavy glass pane, set in the outer wall and encrusted with dust. I dropped the pick and grabbed the Smith-Wesson as a shadow moved across the opening.

The dark blue trousers of the man outside moved to one side, spun crazily as I got one shot off. The crack of the gun made my head sing and powder fumes seemed to fill the cellar. The window starred and splintered and the bullet kicked up a puff of dust near the big

155

man's heels. He went away obliquely, moving fast and I lost him a second later. The girl's anxious voice came up to me as I shifted over but he was now cut off by the edge of the window.

'Did you get him?'

I shook my head. A moment or two later I heard the faint whisper of a car going away down the drive. I turned and clambered down over the crates. I looked at the girl steadily.

'How come you knew it was a man?'

'Obviously the same man who's been coming up here all along,' the girl said calmly. 'This sort of thing isn't woman's work.'

I dusted myself down and sat on a crate where I could see the girl's face clearly.

'He wasn't the man we're after,' I said.

I looked round the cellar.

'This is amateur stuff. A professional wouldn't have locked us in here to start with. There's too many possibilities. And if he had he'd have made sure there was no outside window.'

I looked over toward the sunshine. I could almost feel the fresh air swirling in through the shattered glass.

'And on top of that he would have cut off the electricity.'

I got up again and wandered around among the sheeted furniture.

'It's the reaction of a panicky man faced with a situation he can't handle.'

156

The girl followed me, walking with small, careful steps among the debris on the floor.

'You talk as though you know who's involved, Mike,' she said.

'Maybe I do,' I told her. I kicked thoughtfully at the pick-handle among the debris of abandoned tools.

'A pro. would have made sure all this stuff wasn't here,' I said.

Samantha Fogel's eyes shone.

'Perhaps we could hack our way through the door?' she said.

I smiled. My face started throbbing again.

'And maybe we could blast our way to the moon by tapping the oil lines to the heating plant. Not a chance.'

I looked at the girl's trim figure. She flushed slightly and shifted on the balls of her feet.

'But perhaps I could enlarge the window enough for you to squeeze through. It's worth a try.'

The girl looked from me to the window and then back again dubiously.

'It's two feet thick,' she said.

'Sure,' I said. 'But we need only enlarge the aperture by a few inches. And someone's been doing some concreting at one side. That shouldn't be so difficult to shift as solid granite.'

The girl smiled for the first time since we'd come into the cellar.

'Aren't you afraid I'll slip away and leave

you trapped?' she said.

I shook my head.

'If you'd had anything to do with this you'd have made sure you were on the other side of the door.'

The girl came forward. She stared at me for a moment and then she was in my arms. Her mouth met mine hungrily.

'Just in case we're here a long time, Mike,' she said. 'There's something I've wanted to find out ever since we met.'

I looked round the dusty cellar.

'This is as good a place as any,' I said.

The girl's body was warm and yielding beneath my hands as we rolled over against the crates.

2

Cement dust rained into my face, blinded me. I swung the pick, enlarging the edge of the window; it was more than two inches wider now. Samantha Fogel watched me apprehensively. My body was soaked with perspiration and sweat ran down into my eyes. I stopped, wiped my forehead and put the pick against the wall. Dust swirled in the bright light which came in through the window aperture. I'd only been working for half an hour but it seemed like all day.

'You think we'll make it, Mike?' the girl said

calmly.

I got my handkerchief out and mopped the back of my neck.

'I don't see why not,' I said.

I sounded more confident than I felt. I sat down on one of the crates and got out my package of cigarettes. The girl took two and lit them. She took one out of her mouth and passed it to me. I inhaled the smoke gratefully. The girl went over toward the aperture and scrambled up closer. She inspected it critically.

'Another couple of inches and I could squeeze through, Mike.'

'Maybe,' I said. 'I shall have to clear the glass first. And I can't do that until I'm farther into the wall.'

The atmosphere in the cellar now was heavy and oppressive; the heat seemed to come in from the grounds outside and suck all the energy out of one. The naked bulbs burnt dimly and I noticed the shadows on the floor had shifted. I glanced at my watch. It was already eleven a.m. and it might take hours to break out.

I was lucky to have found the concrete work adjoining the window; the stone blocks alone might have made the task impossible. I wondered for the third or fourth time just why the work had been done at all; though perhaps part of the cellar had collapsed and they couldn't be bothered to replace it with stone.

I wandered over to the carpentry work and

inspected it while I finished my cigarette. I could see now the material flanked a row of newish wine-bins. They were nearly all empty. Presumably the framework had been a continuation of the series which had never been completed. I saw that the timber covered the lower part of the cement-work. I stood there with the perspiration trickling down me and a fly buzzing in the silence, while the girl hovered behind me. Her eyes had a question-mark in them but I didn't dare answer her.

In the end I lifted the pick again and shifted the heavy baulks of timber over. I put them to one side. Standing on top of them I found they made a more solid platform than the jumbled heap of crates. I put my back into the work and the cement chips began to fly. I was closer to the front of the window now, the cement work scarred and gashed. I broke all the glass out of the window and reduced the edges to a dull mass. The right hand side of the embrasure looked a great deal bigger but I knew I could never get through it, even with the enlargement.

The timberwork trembled and I found Samantha Fogel back beside me again. She inspected the opening critically. Her breath was warm and perfumed on the side of my cheek and her hair tickled my ear. It reminded me of an hour ago. The memory was still a little too vivid for comfort. I grinned faintly and turned toward her.

'I think I could make it, Mike,' she said. 'With a little push from behind, that is.'

'Give it a few more minutes, honey,' I said.

I swung the pick again, working back and forth along the depth of the window and then I attacked the wall adjoining the opening. There was a big area of concrete to the right and my pick suddenly went through. I tore it free and large flakes of cement broke away and went pattering down over the jumbled mass of boxes and crates. I stopped then when I saw the dark crack in the surface and the cavity beyond. I shielded the wall with my back and went on enlarging the window area.

The girl went down and got some sacks. I rolled them and padded them round the bottom and right hand side of the window, to protect her from the jagged edges of the glass. She was back up top now, watching my preparations with a pink tongue curling round the edge of her mouth.

'Supposing our visitor's taken the key of the cellar door away with him, Mike?' she said.

I'd thought of that, tried to push it away to the edges of my mind. I grinned.

'You can always feed me through the window,' I said.

Samantha Fogel shook her head, perhaps to hide the worry in her eyes.

'Maybe he left the key,' she said brightly. 'That way it might look more like an accident.'

'Just so long as you come back,' I said.

The girl leaned over and kissed me full on the mouth.

'Try and keep me away,' she said.

She eased her head and shoulders into the window embrasure and wriggled about for a moment. There seemed to be room now. I pushed her gently forward, holding her body round the hips. I heard her grunt as her shoulders met the stone on either side.

'Take it easy,' I said.

I felt, rather than saw her reach forward with her right hand and ease the folds of sacking over the glass.

'If it's too tough come back and try again,' I said.

Her shoulder muscles flexed under the shirt as she shook her head. I heard her breathing heavily. She had both arms up over her head now as she eased forward into what had been the glassed area. The light had nearly all gone from round her body and I saw that despite her slimness it was going to be a tight fit. I could never have done it.

I caught her legs round the knees and took the strain off her muscles. I guided her slowly forward. Cement was cracking away from the right hand wall now, revealing the depths of the cavity I hadn't wanted the girl to see. She gave a convulsive wriggle and for one bleak moment I thought she had stuck. Then she started going forward again, with infinite slowness. I got some more sacking and stuffed

it into the window edge my side, to prevent her knees from rubbing. Only the lower portion of her legs was inside the cellar now. I heard her voice, muffled, but with a note of triumph.

'I'm in the open air, Mike. Another two or three inches should do it.'

She wriggled again and her legs moved forward, more slowly this time. Then she seemed to tense and light streamed in through the window again. I jumped forward and caught her by the back of her belt as she sagged suddenly downward.

'You don't want to break your neck at this stage,' I said.

I felt her body tremble under my hands and then she had apparently taken the weight on her hands. I held the sacking firm over the glass as she slid her legs out. A moment later her smiling face appeared in the window opening.

'Just hold on, Mike.'

'I'm not going anywhere, honey,' I said.

I waited until I heard her footsteps crunch across the gravel. I got down to the foot of the crates then and scrabbled around for the pick. I had perhaps five minutes. I came back up and hacked at the concrete surround to the right of the window. Chips flew and then the tip of the pick had broken through. A great crack ran from floor to ceiling. I peered forward into the cavity.

There was a bundle inside wrapped in

sacking. Somehow I didn't want to touch it with my hand. It collapsed forward as I enlarged the hole. I inserted the thin end of the pick slowly and carefully into the sacking. It was dry and brittle with age and it tore with a high, thin sound that set my nerves on edge. I found myself staring at the wizened, mummified face of a man. Though he was twenty years younger there was no mistaking the resemblance to Adelbert Fogel. Samantha's father had never left home.

CHAPTER SIXTEEN

1

Sweat cascaded down my face as I stood there in the dimness of the cellar. I suddenly heard the sharp, strident call of a cicada from somewhere out in the grounds. A metallic rattling that echoed through the cellar seemed to scald my nerves. I picked up the sacking from the window, draped it over the head of the thing that stood in the alcove and pushed it back into position. My heart was thumping uncomfortably. You're getting old, Faraday, I told myself.

I made it to the cellar steps in three seconds flat as the girl swung the big steel door open. She stood looking down at me, smiling.

'He left the key in the lock,' she said brightly.

'He's an amateur,' I reminded her. 'He's not the one we're after.'

I pushed her back out the cellar, switched off the lights and locked the steel door behind us. I put the key in my pocket. The girl looked at me with a faint frown on her face but she didn't say anything. We got out in the upper cellar and I re-closed the heavy wooden door behind us. We were back in her car before she spoke again. She reversed expertly down the lane and gunned off toward the front entrance to Place of Hawks.

'I take it we've a destination, Mike?'

'Some pieces just clicked into place,' I said. 'I'd like to have a word with Colonel Proctor now. Take the shortest way.'

She didn't say anything else, just concentrated on the driving, spinning the wheel expertly as she tooled the car round the narrow, winding curves. I could see my face in the driving mirror. It looked dirty as well as sardonic now, the hair hanging lankly over my forehead. I looked more like fifty-three than thirty-three. The girl looked as cool and refreshing as though we hadn't spent the morning in the cellar. As well as metaphorically rolling around in the hay.

My face had assumed a satisfied look in the mirror at the recollection. I used my handkerchief to get the dust off and then

165

straightened my hair. I glanced at the girl again. Apart from a few strands of cobweb on the shoulder of her shirt she looked as smart as a fashion plate. She smiled faintly as I put my hand on her shoulder and brushed the cobwebs off.

Dust drifted across the road as Samantha Fogel eased the car round a very sharp curve and on to a T-junction. We nosed out and were then gunning along a stretch of road I recognized. It was about a mile from the main entrance of Place of Hawks. I glanced at my watch. It was lunch-time. Just the right time to hit the Proctor place. The girl turned off the main stem without being told and fought the automobile round the series of S-bends that led up the steep hillside to where Colonel Proctor's big stone house sat smiling in the sunshine.

Samantha drew the car up on the gravelled concourse below the terrace and killed the motor. A silence broken only by the chirping of the cicadas flowed back in. I looked around. The mini was standing baking in the sunshine but there was no sign of the Rolls. I went over to the garage block tunnelled into the hillside. There was a window let into the top of the big door. Apart from some packing cases and a work bench, the garage was empty. Pretty much what I figured. I went back to the girl.

'Stay here and keep your eyes peeled,' I said. 'If the Colonel shows keep him talking

166

until I get back.'

'He might be up at the house,' Samantha Fogel said.

She patted a stray lock of hair.

'He might,' I said. 'I won't be long.'

I took the steps two at a time despite the heat. The terrace was deserted and the big white front door of the house was standing open. I went around the side, walking on the soft grass edging the path, watching where I put my feet, careful not to make a noise. A set of French windows came up at the rear of the house. They were slightly ajar and I could hear low voices and the chinking of glasses coming from inside.

I eased forward until I could see into the room. It was a big one with pale green silk walls and a lot of divans scattered about. I noticed something else too. The blonde girl Caroline sat on one end of the divan facing the window. She was quite nude and her magnificent body had an even golden tan which went all over. She had her legs spread and her hair was cascading back across the cushions. Mrs James was sitting beside her. She wore a red flowered silk dressing gown so I couldn't see what sort of figure she had. The air was full of sweet-smelling cigarette smoke. Smoke was rising from a crystal tray on a low table in front of the divan and there were glasses and bottles on the table top.

When I saw what the two women were

167

doing I knew Proctor wouldn't be around that afternoon. My hair didn't exactly rise on my scalp but it tried. I figured it was a waste of talent. Mrs James raised her head then and kissed the girl on the lips. Caroline's eyes were wide and vacant and her speech slurred. I didn't hang around to hear what they were saying. Proctor was telling the truth about one thing anyway.

I gum-shoed my way back to the front entrance and hit the bell. I had to repeat the toccata and fugue about three times before I heard a rustling noise in back of the hall. Mrs James came shuffling out, adjusting her dressing gown with an expression on her face as livid as hell. She contorted it into something like a smile when she saw me and came forward with her hand held out.

'I'm sorry I didn't hear you at first, Mr Faraday,' she said in a low voice. 'I was lying down in rear of the house. These hot afternoons, you know.'

'It does get pretty hot up here,' I said.

Mrs James shot a sharp glance at me but she couldn't read anything on my face.

'You'll be wanting Henry, I suppose?'

'That was the general idea,' I said.

Mrs James wasn't looking so elegant this afternoon. Some of the tinting had faded from her hair and I could see the grey in the roots. But she still moved and looked pretty good, though the frost at my interruption was never

far from the edges of her voice. She pulled the robe across her finely contoured breasts as though she could read some of my thoughts. It was a pretty hot afternoon now I came to think of it.

'He's gone away,' she said sharply, half-turning to look over my shoulder at the distant hills.

'It doesn't surprise me,' I said. 'When are you expecting him back?'

Mrs James wrinkled up her face like the sun was hurting her eyes.

'It's quite a longish trip,' she said. 'He'll be out of town some time.'

'When you contact him,' I said, 'you might tell him the game is up. He'll probably phone in to see if I've been around.'

Mrs James looked bewildered but a chalky colour had started flooding into her complexion. She stared at me. Some of the dope was clearing from her eyes.

'I don't think I follow you, Mr Faraday.'

'The Colonel will understand,' I said.

I stared at her for a long moment. She was the first to drop her eyes.

'And I think you do too,' I said.

I turned on my heel and left her without saying goodbye. The cloying, hothouse atmosphere of the place was suddenly too much for me. And I had the girl on my mind. It was going to be tough breaking it to her about her father. I'd meet that later. Right

now I had to get in touch with old man Fogel without tipping off Pushkin's heavies.

I went down the steps two at a time. Samantha Fogel had turned the car and parked it farther down. She was up at the far end of the terrace looking at the terrain down below through the big telescope. The cat I'd seen before was stretched out on the paving eying her with lazy yellow eyes. Samantha turned round and came back down the paving toward me as she heard my footsteps. She made her way down to the concourse. We met by the bonnet of the car.

'You probably think I'm crazy, Sam,' I said. 'But I'd like you to come on into L.A. with me. If you can spare the time.'

The girl looked at me gravely.

'I can spare the time, Mike,' she said. 'It's about my father, isn't it?'

I nodded. The girl shaded her eyes from the sun with the edge of her hand.

'You're on to something?'

'Could be,' I said. 'I don't want to raise too many hopes but some of the ends of this business are coming into my hands. I'd like you to be around when I question old man Fogel. Your knowledge could be useful.'

'What about your car?' the girl said.

'We can pick that up tomorrow,' I said. 'Right now I feel it's important to get back into L.A. You can stay with my secretary tonight. She'll be able to find you some things.'

'I'm not worried about that,' Samantha Fogel said. 'If you think it will help.'

'It will help a lot,' I said.

The girl got behind the wheel of the car with a lithe, sinuous movement.

'I'd like to ring my mother and tell her where we've gone,' she said.

'We'll find a phone on the way,' I said. 'Besides, it's past lunch-time and I'm hungry.'

The girl grinned. She switched on the motor and sat waiting for me to get in the passenger seat. The sun felt hot and heavy on my shoulder blades as I stood there on the concourse and looked back up at Colonel Proctor's dream palace. I wondered what Mrs James was saying to Caroline right now. Something unprintable, I guessed.

'You won't say anything to your mother about this?' I said as I got into the car.

The shadow came back into Samantha Fogel's eyes as she started tooling the car back down the S-bends toward the road.

'I won't say a word,' she said. 'Besides, you haven't told me anything yet. Other than that you might have a line on my father. He's dead, isn't he?'

I couldn't look at her for a moment but she must have read the expression in my eyes.

'You knew that anyway, didn't you?' I said.

She nodded, her hair whipped back by the wind coming in the car window. We were opposite Place of Hawks now and she turned

the car, running it alongside the high wall of the estate. That wall was like a lot of fences people put round their lives, to hide their secret thoughts and emotions.

The girl smiled again. She turned toward me, moving slightly in the driving seat.

'You're right, Mike,' she said. 'Father went away a long time ago. It's just that it would help if we could know one way or another.'

'You'll know soon,' I promised her.

She didn't say any more but settled down to the driving. We started making time toward L.A.

2

The office was blue with tobacco smoke. Stella sat opposite me, the lamplight shining on the gold bell of her hair. She looked from me to Samantha Fogel and then back again.

'The coffee's good,' I said, picking up my second cup.

I reached for my cigarette butt on the earthenware tray in front of me. My voice was hoarse with talking. I'd filled in the two girls on the last couple of days. Omitting any mention of the corpse in the cellar, of course. There would be time for that.

'The dark-haired man's name was Tony Reno,' Stella said. 'It was in the papers. He had a record as long as the freeway tunnel. So

I shouldn't lose any sleep.'

'I won't,' I said.

Stella grinned faintly at Samantha Fogel. She sat in a chair opposite me, cupping her beaker of coffee and trying to catch up on the dialogue.

'I take it the police weren't looking for me?' I said.

Stella shook her head. 'They put it down to another mob killing. So no one came around.'

'Just as well,' I said. 'You get any line on Reno?'

There was an expression of quiet triumph in Stella's eyes. She leaned forward and flipped over a cardboard folder on the desk in front of her.

'He was a bouncer at a place called the Astor Club,' she said. 'I looked up the address for you.'

I had a sudden glimpse of Reno's dying face in the yard before I lit out through the back way.

'He muttered something about Astor before he kicked off,' I said.

'That's it, then,' Stella said. 'It shouldn't take you long to shake a little information out of Moses Pushkin. You turn right at Wiltshire . . .'

'I know, honey,' I said. 'Not five miles from where we're sitting. Big Sam must have done some doubling while I was blindfolded.'

Stella turned to Samantha Fogel

apologetically.

'You mustn't mind us, Miss Fogel. It's like this all the time when we're working. I'll bone you up on the details later.'

Samantha Fogel smiled lazily like she was tired.

'I'm perfectly happy right here,' she said. 'I'll leave it all to you and Mr Faraday. As long as we find out something about Place of Hawks. Who goes up there and why. And what happened to my father.'

'We'll find out,' I said.

I got up and went over to the window. I put my hand on the girl's shoulder for a moment as I went by. Stella drank her coffee and looked at Samantha sympathetically.

'I'm all through here if you're going to take Sam on home,' I told Stella. 'She'll probably want to buy some things if you're going across town.'

'Is that a hint to get rid of us?' Stella said.

'Not at all,' I said. 'The heat's off now, anyway.'

Samantha Fogel got up with that lazy movement I found so attractive.

'What will you be doing?' Stella said dubiously.

'I think I'll take a look over at the Astor Club,' I told her.

CHAPTER SEVENTEEN

1

The Astor Club was a large brick box that had
seen better days. One of the neons that spelled
out the club's name was cracked and some of
the stucco peeling from the walls. But it
looked pretty crowded when I drove Samantha
Fogel's heap by and turned in the alley that I
figured would lead to the rear of the premises.
The layout was exactly as I remembered from
my walk with Big Sam. I killed the motor and
broke out the Smith-Wesson.

I threw off the safety and gum-shoed
through the door and along the stretch of grey
carpet which I remembered from my previous
visit. The monotonous beat of the far-off band
went on somewhere beyond the doors which
led off the corridor. I turned right at the end
of the passage like I'd been used to this place
all my life. There was no-one around and no
sound coming from behind the walnut doors
which lined the corridor.

I went quickly up the narrow stairway with
the wrought iron railing and through the
walnut door facing the stairs which had Private
on it in gold. I'd expected it to be unlocked
and the knob turned smoothly in my hand. I
had the Smith-Wesson in my right, pointed

straight ahead, and I got through the door as quickly and quietly as possible.

Dim lamps burned in the big office with panelled walls. It appeared to be empty. I locked the door quietly behind me and went on over the thick carpet. The marble fireplace and the sporting prints were just as I remembered them. I waited a moment to get my bearings in the dusk and to adjust my eyes to the lowered intensity of the lighting. A tiny muscle fretted in my cheek. I could hear a faint regular sound like breathing coming from somewhere in the room.

The thick drapes were drawn over the long windows which made it more difficult to see. I moved over toward the wall and worked my way slowly along, my movements muffled by the deep pile carpet. I made out the sound. It was unusual for a place like the Astor Club. It was a man sobbing. I spotted the hunched figure then, almost invisible against the black covering of a large divan which stretched between two of the windows. I lifted the Smith-Wesson and stepped closer.

Big Sam moved slowly, his enormous body rocking with grief. He held his massive hands over his head and I could see tears glisten as they trickled through his fingers.

'This may not be the best time but I'd like a word with Pushkin,' I said gently.

The big man pulled down his hands from his face and looked at me like he didn't recognize

me. His eyes were glazed and the lids reddened. The spectacle was so incongruous that I just stood there without saying anything. Big Sam made a convulsive movement. Recognition flooded into his eyes. He made as though to get up.

'Just sit where you are, Sam,' I said. 'I can't take any chances with a character your size. I've got five in the Smith-Wesson. Enough to stop even you. So just take it easy.'

Big Sam wiped his eyes with the knuckles of his hands and squirmed upward on the divan.

'You got nothing to fear from me, Mr Faraday,' he said in a muffled voice. 'I didn't rough you up last time, did I?'

I put one foot on the end of the divan and rested the barrel of the Smith-Wesson on my knee. The muzzle was pointed steadily at his chest and I let it stay there.

'No you did not, Sam,' I agreed. 'And for that I am grateful. I don't hold any grudge. I already settled with Tony Reno.'

The big man cracked a slight grin. With his tear-streaked face he looked like the show-stopper in Pagliacci.

'I read about that,' he said. 'I told him to lay off but he never took no notice.'

'Something's upset you, Sam,' I said. 'That's none of my business. I've got no quarrel with you. I just want a word with Pushkin.'

Big Sam stared stonily at me for a moment or two longer. His dark brown suit looked like

it had been slept in and his hammered sheet-metal face looked grey and dead except for the eyes. They were burning with misery.

'You come too late, Mr Faraday,' he said in a bleak voice. 'Somebody got to him first. I found him half an hour ago.'

He jerked his thumb toward the door of the inner office.

'Go take a look if you don't believe me.'

'After you, Sam, if you don't mind,' I said, taking my foot down from the divan and gesturing him up with the gun. 'It's not that I don't trust you but I'd be a sucker to leave a fellow your size in rear of me.'

Sam nodded slowly like the idea hadn't occurred to him. He looked the oddest sight I'd ever seen. And yet he was somehow dignified in his grief. His tea-cup handle ears stood out against the dark curtains as he got hesitantly to his feet. His bulk filled the whole room as he loomed over me. Our shadows crawled across the ceiling as we went across the office. Big Sam opened the door and beckoned me through. We went on in.

2

Like before the floor-to-ceiling drapes in Pushkin's office were pulled. Our feet were muffled on the carpet as we went across toward his massive desk. One of the white

178

leather bar stools was lying over on its side on the floor like someone had gotten up in a hurry. There were two empty glasses lying on the polished surface of the bar counter. Just now I wasn't interested in the decor though.

Big Sam stepped to one side as we got up to the desk and spread out his hands in a helpless gesture. I lowered the gun and stepped round him. Pushkin sat bolt upright in his swivel chair behind the desk with a fixed smile on his face. There were specks of blood on some of the papers on the blotter in front of him. Otherwise things looked fairly normal if you overlooked the grey waxen colour of his skin.

He wore the uniform white tie and tails and it wasn't until I got up quite close that I could see the patch of congealed blood under the lapels of his cutaway. I could smell powder smoke now. Big Sam went and sat on one of the bar stools and looked at me morosely. I didn't say anything. I walked around the desk, being careful where I put my feet. There was quite a lot of blood on the carpet.

Pushkin's black eyebrows were arched in surprise and there were tiny flecks of blood in the roots of his silver-grey hair. His fleshy lips were drawn back over the white, square teeth in a rictus that was painful to look at. I got around the desk and stopped. I could see the big hole blown in the back of the leather chair now. The killer had put the muzzle right up against the leather and the edges of the hole

179

and part of the padding were scorched and buckled by the flash.

Whoever used a .45 on him must have blown his backbone clean out; all the damage was concealed by the chairback. I didn't look any further.

'You see anyone come up here?' I asked Big Sam.

'Seven or eight guys came up this evening,' he said. 'Daddy Pushkin told me to get lost. Said he had a character coming who was going to repay a lot of money. I went down in the bar for an hour.'

I nodded. I went around the bar and rummaged on a shelf and found two glasses. I poured a big shot for me and a bigger one for Sam. He emptied it in one gulp and slid the glass back for a re-fill. I took my own glass and went and sat in the chair the other side of the desk and looked at Pushkin thoughtfully.

'He must have trusted whoever did it,' I said.

Big Sam looked at me with a stupid expression on his face.

'How you figure that, Mr Faraday?'

'To let somebody get behind him like that,' I said. 'Maybe he was writing something.'

I had an idea then.

'You know where Pushkin kept his safe keys?'

Big Sam brightened visibly. He was halfway through his second glass by now.

'He always kept the keys on him,' he said. 'You want me to find out?'

'I shouldn't touch him,' I said.

I went around the desk again, walking in a wide arc.

'We shall have to wash these glasses before we blow,' I told the big man. 'Just leave the other two glasses for the law.'

Big Sam nodded and shifted his bulk on the bar-stool.

'Somebody owed Daddy Pushkin money and cancelled the debt the hard way,' he told the panelled walls.

'I figured it wasn't just for the fudge-concession at Ocean Beach,' I said.

I spotted the open safe-door then. The picture had been slid aside and papers were hanging out. I sighed. As a case it was getting heavier and heavier. I went over and looked inside. There were some thick ledgers on the bottom shelf. Probably the killer hadn't time to clear everything. I looked at Big Sam. He was still sitting on the bar-stool, swilling his drink. I indicated the safe.

'You don't mind?' I said.

'Be my guest,' the big man said.

I put the Smith-Wesson away and examined the papers. They were all IOU's for big amounts, some of them up to 50,000 dollars and more. I figured the killer had taken only the stuff relating to himself. I lifted out the ledger and took it over to the divan and spread

it on my knee. The names were arranged in alphabetical order. That of Fogel seemed to leap out of the page at me. I sat back and closed up the book. Something like a great sheet of light seemed to flood into the room. I felt like laughing out loud only that would have been disrespectful to the dead.

'Looks like I've been looking at things from the wrong angle,' I told the silent figure of Pushkin. Big Sam didn't say anything. He got up and came quietly over and put his hand out for my glass. I gave it to him. He went back behind the bar and started to rinse it in the sink. I stood looking at Pushkin and then swivelled back to Sam.

'You're finished here,' I told the big gorilla.

He looked at me sadly. 'Everything finishes,' he said.

He put the glasses back on the shelf with a grunt.

'I got a brother in Detroit,' he said.

'I should visit him,' I told him.

Big Sam grinned suddenly.

'Got you,' he said.

He faded silently but the room and I heard the leather-padded door shut softly behind him. I went round the office turning off the lights, using my handkerchief to handle the switches. Then I got the hell out too.

CHAPTER EIGHTEEN

1

The bungalow I wanted was on a lonely piece of real estate off Coldwater Drive. I'd got outside a barbecued beef sandwich when I left Pushkin's place and then I rang Stella. I put her in the picture and asked her to do some address checking for me. I stayed in the booth until she rang back. I jotted down the details she gave me and then asked for Samantha Fogel. The girl's voice sounded tinny and far away like there was some impediment on the line.

'You all right, Sam?' I said.

'Sure, Mike. Stella's been telling me a lot of things about you.'

'I'll bet,' I said. 'There's just one question I want to ask.'

'Any way I can help,' she said.

'Something's been puzzling me,' I said. 'About the way your father disappeared, I mean. I know you were in Europe at the time and only a child but you must have gone into it many times since.'

'Sure,' Samantha Fogel said. 'Just what is it you want to know?'

'When your father disappeared where was your family?'

'That's simple,' Samantha Fogel said. 'Place of Hawks was shut up. My mother, my brother, who now practises law in San Francisco, and the staff had left on vacation. My father said there was something he had to see to. He stayed behind and was to join them the following day.'

'So he walked out his office in L.A. that night and disappeared,' I said.

'That's about it,' Samantha Fogel said. 'Does that answer your query? Though I can't see its importance.'

'You've just given me the last piece, honey,' I said. 'Everything else fits. I can't talk now. Put Stella back on, will you?'

I told Stella where I was going and why. She took notes as I rattled on. A frosty-faced woman hovering outside the booth holding two poodles on a twin leash gave me a flash of some expensive bridgework as she scowled in my direction. I kept on talking.

'It'll take me a half-hour to get there,' I said. 'Give me two hours. If you haven't heard anything by then ring the law. He's already killed once tonight.'

I made sure Stella had got the details down like I'd told her.

'Not a word to the Fogel girl,' I said. 'I'll tell her about her father myself.'

'You sure you won't wait for the police, Mike?' Stella said.

'There isn't time,' I said. 'Besides, all I've

got is theory. I've got to make him crack my way. To do that I need time.'

'All right,' Stella said. 'Just take care, that's all.'

'I've got something that will give teeth to the argument if talk fails,' I said.

I said goodbye to Stella and rang off. The matron in the mauve and green flowered hat made an audible clicking noise with her tongue as she scuttled into the booth. I grinned and went on out. I was still driving Samantha Fogel's sport-job and I stopped halfway across town to gas up. A thin rain was starting to fall as I hit Coldwater Canyon and searched for the turning I wanted.

I found the bungalow, a substantial Spanish-style property with balconies and big dormer windows that really turned it into a two-storey place. I pulled the car in on to a well-shaved strip of turf between two palms and killed the motor. I sat listening to the soft swish of rain on the car roof and checked the Smith-Wesson in the dim light of the dash-lamps. I threw off the safety and put the gun back in the holster.

Then I killed the sidelights and eased out of the car, closing the door quietly behind me. I walked up through the big white-painted gates that were thrown back in two wide wings like they were welcoming the visitor. A light burned in a brass lantern set atop a pole by the gateway. The nearest house was about twenty yards away and concealed behind high hedges.

There were lights burning somewhere in rear of the bungalow because I could see the illumination thrown in square rectangles on the grass. I got on the lawn that edged the driveway to avoid walking on the red gravel. There were two cars standing in front of the glassed-in porch of the front entrance. I went up the steps, opened the porch door and walked quietly through until I got to the doorway proper. I could smell the sweet, cloying smell of hot-house plants as I thumbed the button.

2

There was a long silence. The sound of the rain on the roof and the foliage surrounding the house made a melancholy background to my thoughts. I thumbed the button again. This time light sprang up in the bungalow though the porch was still dim. The door was opened on a chain. There was a shadowy face in the opening. The voice sounded hesitant.

'Yes?'

'Mr Fogel?' I said. 'Faraday. I'd like a little talk. We met at the office, remember?'

The chain was rattling, the door opening. I started to step in, changed my mind. I went at the panel full tilt, slamming it back with my shoulder. Fogel gave a high, shrill yelp as the door caught him across the face. He was

propelled backwards into the hallway, cannoning off the wall. Something big and heavy thumped on to the carpet. I got to the light switch by this time.

I slammed the door to behind me, stooped and picked up the cannon Fogel had dropped. It was a .45. I held it by the barrel and sniffed it. My guess was it had been recently fired.

The young man in the blue dressing gown sprawled at my feet had a sullen look on his face. Blood trickled down his cheek from a cut over his forehead. He got to his feet with barely-suppressed fury. His face was white with rage and a vein in his forehead was bulging.

'Are you mad, Faraday? What the hell do you mean by busting in here like this? I'll get my father to bounce you off your licence.'

'I don't think you'll do anything, Mr Fogel,' I said. 'Not after I hand this gun to the police.'

I wrapped the pistol in my handkerchief and put it in my pocket. Fogel bit his lip and moved forward until he was brought up sharply by the sight of the Smith-Wesson in my left.

'I'm right-handed but I couldn't fail to splatter your gut if you start anything,' I said.

Fogel passed a blue tongue round the corner of his mouth. His eyes looked hunted as he fought to regain normality.

'You're a private dick,' he said sullenly. 'You've no right here.'

'Perfectly true,' I said. 'But since you were

ready to use that cannon on me a minute ago I'd say it was time to drop the formalities.'

I gestured with the Smith-Wesson barrel and motioned Fogel forward. He straightened his crumpled dressing gown with a slight shrug and went in through the far door. It was a big room, tastefully furnished, with low-key lighting, a few good paintings, and divans with cushions scattered about. It looked what it was; a young man's fancy pad. I looked around for female underwear but couldn't see any.

'You alone?' I said.

Alex Fogel took a pack of cigarettes out his pocket and lit one with a trembling hand. Some of the sneer had gotten back into his voice when he answered.

'Any reason I shouldn't be?'

'None at all,' I said.

I noted a thin wisp of smoke going up from the stone ashtray on the desk at the side of the fireplace. The heavy drapes at the window were drawn.

'Let's stop playing games, Mr Fogel,' I said. 'You know why I'm here. There's just a few pieces I need now and it's all wrapped up.'

'You don't make sense to me, Faraday,' Fogel said harshly. He went over to the desk and picked up a half-full glass of whisky which was standing on its green leather surface.

'I guess I'd better spell it out for you, then,' I said.

I went over and squatted on the edge of the

desk. Fogel sat down in a black leather chair almost opposite me. I kept the Smith-Wesson steady on his gut. His limbs had stopped trembling now and some of the colour was coming back into his face. His dark black hair was still parted symmetrically. The bleeding from the cut had stopped now. The thin blackish trickle looked like a continuation of his hairline. His white teeth flashed brilliantly as he took another pull at the whisky.

'I'd offer you one but this isn't a social occasion,' he said.

'You can say that again,' I said. 'Let's take a hypothetical case of a young man with a lot of expensive tastes and a shortage of money. He likes gambling, booze and girls. He's in a rich business too. There's only one snag. His father's almost a miser who keeps tight strings on the money-bags.'

Fogel cupped his hands round his glass and sat back in the chair, regarding me steadily.

'You haven't said anything that isn't public knowledge.'

'This is how I read the story,' I said. 'Correct me if I'm wrong. The young man is a compulsive gambler. He gets in way over his head. I'm going back ten years, of course. He'd only be around twenty-two then. Even more impulsive and silly than he is now.'

Fogel was gripping his glass with stiffened fingers. He didn't say anything so I went on.

'Try this for size. He gets in too deep,

189

gambles away funds that he's no right to. He's in one of the biggest and most lucrative law practices in L.A. His father may be a tightwad but he's honest and doesn't approve of the son's way of life. The uncle, Charles Fogel is also a man of honour. And being a man of honour, he decides to give his nephew a chance when he discovers deficits in the accounts.'

I looked at Fogel steadily, beating him down with my gaze.

'That was the set-up, wasn't it?' I said. 'How much?'

Fogel sank his head on his chest. He looked defeated and dejected. His voice was so low when he replied that I could hardly hear him.

'Way over a hundred thousand dollars,' he said.

I nodded. 'You were desperate. You pleaded with your uncle. He promised to meet you at Place of Hawks to discuss the matter. You chose a night when you knew the family had gone on holiday. And Charles Fogel walked out of his office that night to disappear for ever.'

Fogel took another sip at his glass. Strength had come back into his voice.

'It was simple really,' he said. 'And fool-proof. I argued with the old idiot. I could see it was no use. He would have exposed me to my father. My career, the money and my hopes of a senior partnership would have gone for

good. I got tired of arguing with him. No one knew we were meeting. And the house is a lonely place, as you know. So I shot him. It was a Friday night. I had all the time in the world.'

I got off the desk and took a turn around the room, watching Fogel carefully. The curtains belled slightly with the movement of the night wind.

'So you took him down to the cellar and cemented him into the wall,' I said.

There was a crash. I looked up quickly. Fogel's glass was rolling across the carpet. The whites of his eyes showed as he stared at me.

'How did you know that?' he whispered.

'I dug him up this morning,' I said. 'Your man blew it.'

Fogel shook his head. His eyes looked dark and tired.

'It figures,' he said.

'Talking of Colonel Proctor,' I told him. 'What was his angle? Blackmail?'

Fogel shrugged.

'Let's both have a drink,' he said. 'I might as well tell you everything.'

3

I held up my glass to the light and squinted through it at Fogel. He stood at the sideboard pouring another. I kept the gun on him until he got back to his chair.

'I was out of luck,' he said. 'Colonel Proctor was scouting the area. He was looking for a piece of real estate up there, somewhere near his old friend Adelbert Fogel's place. He saw the lights and chose that night of all nights to call. The front door was unlocked.'

'It must have been a great shock to the Colonel's system,' I said.

Fogel crossed his legs in the elegant blue pyjamas. He seemed to go in for blue. He shook his head.

'The Colonel's an opportunist. That night he became my partner. In return for his silence he took a cut in my business.'

'Very nice for him,' I said. 'I hope it was worth it.'

'He was very useful,' Fogel said. 'He helped me cement the body in. We stayed there all week-end so there was plenty of time to clear up.'

'That's how he built the house opposite,' I said. 'Silence comes high.'

'It was either that or hang,' Fogel said. 'It seemed like a good arrangement at the time. No one knew where Samantha's father had gone and Proctor was pretty smart. He kept an eye on the house once he got his own place built and kept tabs on who came and went.'

'That's why you could never sell it,' I said.

Fogel looked a crushed, sad figure for a moment as he stared at me over the rim of his glass and I had a fleeting stab of pity. It didn't

last more than a second though.

'How did you get away with it?' I said. 'The money, I mean.'

Fogel grinned shyly. His expression seemed strange under those circumstances.

'Fogel handles enormous sums of money,' he said. 'I've been juggling the books for more than ten years. I'm an old hand. We've got more than fifteen millionaires' estates to handle alone. I transfer funds as needed.'

'Pretty sweet,' I said. 'How did you explain the cellar?'

'There was no need,' Fogel said. 'No one ever went into the lower one, which was why I used it.'

'And later you had the steel door put up,' I said. 'That was when the blind aunt moved in.'

A sullen expression crossed Fogel's face again.

'I couldn't talk father out of it,' he said. 'That was one of the worst moments. He was always trying to sell it. He couldn't understand why I wanted to hang on to it.'

'Because one day someone might dig up the thing in the cellar,' I said. 'You poor son of a bitch.'

Fogel swirled the whisky in his glass moodily.

'There have been a few bad moments,' he said.

'Everything was all right until my aunt died.'

'Then Proctor reported seeing lights and

cars at an empty house?' I said.

Fogel nodded. 'That really frightened me. I told Proctor to keep his eyes open. I equipped the kitchen up there and camped out sometimes, trying to find out who the prowler was. But I never did. I started to build some wine racks over the concrete work on the wall.'

'It was Samantha Fogel,' I said. 'You never fooled her. She always suspected her father was dead. And she knew Place of Hawks had something to do with it.'

Fogel looked white. I tightened my grip on the Smith-Wesson. For one moment I thought he was going to get up out of his chair.

'Only we got it all wrong,' I said. 'She thought it was old man Fogel and I tagged along until I saw a ledger entry at the Astor with your name in. You made a big mistake having the oil-tank filled regularly. I hope you didn't send your father the bills.'

'I paid those myself,' Fogel said. He had a quiet air of smugness about him now, as though he was enjoying telling me about himself.

'Everything went fine for a long time. Dad kept crabbing about letting the estate lie idle, so I pretended I was spending all my weekends up there.'

'Something went wrong,' I said. 'Which was when I was called in.'

Fogel nodded. 'Proctor bungled it again. He rang the office one afternoon to tell me he'd

seen someone snooping around the place. Due to a mistake he was put through to my father and blurted out everything before he realized.'

'Which alarmed the old man,' I said. 'No wonder you were startled when I turned up at the office. Why did you put Pushkin on to me?'

Fogel shook his head.

'That wasn't my doing, Mr Faraday. I was into him for a lot of money. I had a run of bad luck at the Astor. I owed him 50,000 dollars.'

I shook my head. 'When you rubbed him you took the IOU's from the safe. But you forgot the ledgers. They say you owe Pushkin 150,000.'

Fogel spread out his left hand in a gesture of resignation.

'He won't be collecting now,' he said. 'Pushkin roughed you because you were threatening his interests. If I went up he lost his money. It was as simple as that.'

'I was late but I figured that about an hour or two ago,' I said.

Fogel laughed a harsh, unconvincing laugh.

'Don't blame yourself, Mr Faraday. This was a tangle. You had no way of knowing what was involved.'

'Nice of you to say so,' I said.

'When Pushkin's diplomacy failed they put the heavies on. After Tony Reno you decided you'd be a little more subtle. You rang up Place of Hawks to give Proctor his

instructions. You spoke to me instead.'

Fogel smiled a tight smile.

'The law of averages,' he said. 'Even I have a few failures now and then. Proctor must have lost his nerve. A dumb play. Locking you in the cellar with the girl.'

'About what I figured,' I said. 'I thought he was being helpful but he turned up to make sure I wouldn't find out anything important.'

'How did you know it was Proctor?' Fogel said.

I got up from the desk and went over to sit in an armchair opposite Fogel.

'He signalled the shots all the way,' I said. 'If you'd phoned Place of Hawks it had to be someone conveniently placed. Proctor's house was the only one for miles around. I saw a heavily built man's lower half pass the cellar window. And then I heard tyres crunching down the drive but no motor. It had to be a Rolls.'

Fogel smiled a twisted grin.

'Proctor blew it all right,' he said.

'You've spoken to him, I take it?' I said. 'He won't get very far. You don't happen to know where he is?'

Fogel shook his head.

'He wouldn't be behind that curtain?' I said.

There was a flash of flame and something fanned my cheek as I flung myself down.

CHAPTER NINETEEN

1

The slap of the explosion seemed to sting my cheeks as I hit the floor and rolled over. I had the Smith-Wesson up and snapped off a shot as the curtains billowed. Fogel had pushed his chair over backwards when the firing began and I heard him crash into something as I kept rolling. I saw him get up but I wasn't worried about him for the moment.

The gun blammed again from behind the curtains and a long sliver of wood hummed off a teak bureau about three feet from me. I was on my feet and dived along the floor aiming for the curtains. There was a high-pitched gasp as I hit someone's legs with my shoulder. We went down in a flailing mass of arms, legs and curtaining. I was chopping through the curtains with the Smith-Wesson barrel, felt the metal connect.

The curtains collapsed as the big Police Special fell to the floor. I turned as the door opened. Alex Fogel was halfway through when I got off my second shot with the Smith-Wesson. I aimed low and I saw him jerk as he got through the door. He kept on going though and a moment later I heard the front door of the bungalow open.

I swore and tore at the curtaining. The blonde hair of Fogel's secretary Dilys spilled through. Her eyes were glazed but she still had enough fight left to spit in my eye. I clamped my hand over her wrist and stopped her from getting to the butt of the Police Special. She stopped struggling and I helped her up. I clicked my teeth.

'I thought Colonel Proctor hadn't got that much stuff in him,' I said.

The girl swore. It wasn't pretty to hear. She wore a leather raincoat with big brass buttons. It had come unbelted in the struggle. She was nude underneath except for a black bra and black pants. She looked pretty good. I shook my head.

'I though your interests and Fogel's were confined to sailing,' I said.

The girl raked my cheek with her nails. I shoved her back into the curtains and scooped up the big revolver. I ran out through the open door of the bungalow. The blood trail wasn't hard to follow. The Smith-Wesson makes a big hole at close quarters. Fogel was lying in the rain, holding a handkerchief round his calf to staunch the flow. His face was twisted with pain. His left hand was stretched up through the open door of the sedan, just short of the ignition. I reached in and took the keys.

'You wouldn't have got far anyway,' I said. 'You'll need a doctor for that.'

'Guess you're right, Mr Faraday,' he said.

Fogel looked at me for a long moment. Then he nodded. There was a strange expression on his face.

I got my hand under his armpit and helped him to his feet. I got him into the bungalow and out of the rain again. I poured him a whisky and left him on the divan. Like I figured the girl was gone. The curtains billowed open in the night wind. Her dress was still lying on the floor in the alcove. I grinned. I heard a car start up in front of the house then.

'It doesn't matter,' I said, in answer to Fogel's unspoken question. 'She wasn't very important. And we can always pick her up any time. Proctor too.'

Fogel didn't say anything, just sat staring down into his glass. I went over to the phone and got Stella and told her what had happened. Then I rang County Police H.Q. I got through to Captain Dan Tucker and told him who I was and where I was and why.

'Look, Mike,' he said. 'We've had some of this before . . .'

'Just drag your underwear over here and make sure you're inside it,' I told him.

I put the phone down. Then I went over and poured myself another drink. It had been quite an evening.

2

Sunlight streamed in through the blinds of the office. The fan was working nicely and I had my second cup of coffee on the blotter. Stella sat with her hands cupped round her own beaker and looked at me quizzically. The sunlight burnished the bell of her hair to liquid gold.

'Hadn't you better tell her, Mike?' she said gently. 'Before the whole thing gets released to the press? You can't keep this under wraps much longer.'

'I'll drive up and break it to her and her mother tonight,' I said.

Stella looked at me steadily. 'She's fond of you, isn't she?'

'I forgot to ask,' I said.

Stella was about to answer when the phone buzzed. She put down her coffee and picked up the instrument. She sat listening for more than a minute.

'I'll tell him,' she said. 'Just as soon as he comes in.'

I could hear a voice raised to a high pitch. Stella grinned.

'I'll tell him that too,' she said.

'The girl Dilys just phoned in,' she said. 'She wants to make a statement. That was Captain Tucker.'

'I thought I recognized that superb diction,' I said. 'What else did he say?'

'He told me to tell you he was doing his best to prevent you from being bounced off your licence,' Stella said sweetly.

'I'll bet,' I said.

Stella looked at me pityingly.

'You brought this one in a bit late, Mike.'

'About the last hour,' I said modestly. 'That was cutting it close even for me.'

Stella snorted.

'And all the time you thought the Colonel was being helpful. All he was doing was keeping tabs on you and making sure you didn't find anything important at Place of Hawks.'

'Don't rub it in, honey,' I said.

'If Proctor hadn't been caught at the Mex border you would have been in real trouble with Alex Fogel denying everything,' Stella said.

I shook my head. I held out my cup for a refill.

'I doubt it, honey,' I said. 'He can hardly deny the corpse at the house. And the slug in Pushkin matches his gun. Proctor blabbing only simplifies things.'

'Anyway, Captain Tucker said you were in real trouble this time,' Stella said.

She put the cup down on my blotter and halfheartedly evaded my probing fingers.

'He always says that,' I told her.

I sat on smoking, watching the bright bars of sunlight stencilled across the floor and thinking about the toughness of a man like Fogel who'd taken the news about his son with a cast-iron façade. Human nature never ceased to surprise me. The phone buzzed again as I raised the cup to my lips. I recognized the voice this time. The rusty-tin buzz went on as Stella struggled to maintain her composure.

'I'll tell him, Mr Fogel,' she said.

She turned to me, putting her hand over the mouthpiece.

'Old man Fogel got our account this morning,' she said. 'He's querying a dollar for iodine and band-aids.'

'Tell him to knock it out,' I said. 'Christmas is only eight months off.'

Stella turned back to the phone and gave the old boy a cleaned-up version of my message. By the crackling noises Fogel made in the receiver I figured he was laying an egg. Stella put the phone back with heaving shoulders.

'He's sending the cheque over by special messenger,' she said. 'Before you change your mind.'

'That's how those guys make their dough,' I said. 'Chopping a dollar out here and there.'

'You didn't tell him the band-aids were for his son,' Stella said.

'What's the point?' I told her.

I finished my coffee and got up and went

out. It was a long drive up to the girl's place and I went around to the garage and gassed up the Buick. I figured to cut off before I got to Place of Hawks. The house would still be swarming with police.

I drove across town and set the car bonnet up into the hills. I wondered if there was some easy way to break the news to Sam and her mother. Or whether I'd taken up the wrong profession. I get like this about once or twice on every heavy case. And they seem to be coming heavier in recent years.

I lit a cigarette and inhaled the smoke, flipping the match stalk out through the open window of the car, enjoying the air on my face and idly watching the flight of a buzzard over the foothills. I gave it up in the end and concentrated on the driving. There's no easy way in my racket. There never is.

We hope you have enjoyed this Large Print book. Other Chivers Press or Thorndike Press Large Print books are available at your library or directly from the publishers.

For more information about current and forthcoming titles, please call or write, without obligation, to:

Chivers Large Print
published by BBC Audiobooks Ltd
St James House, The Square
Lower Bristol Road
Bath BA2 3BH
UK
email: bbcaudiobooks@bbc.co.uk
www.bbcaudiobooks.co.uk

OR

Thorndike Press
295 Kennedy Memorial Drive
Waterville
Maine 04901
USA
www.gale.com/thorndike
www.gale.com/wheeler

All our Large Print titles are designed for easy reading, and all our books are made to last.